THE USBORNE BOOK OF
MACHINES THAT WORK

Caroline Young and Harriet Castor

Designed by Steve Page and Robert Walster

Illustrated by Chris Lyon, Sean Wilkinson, Teri Gower and Nick Hawken

Contents

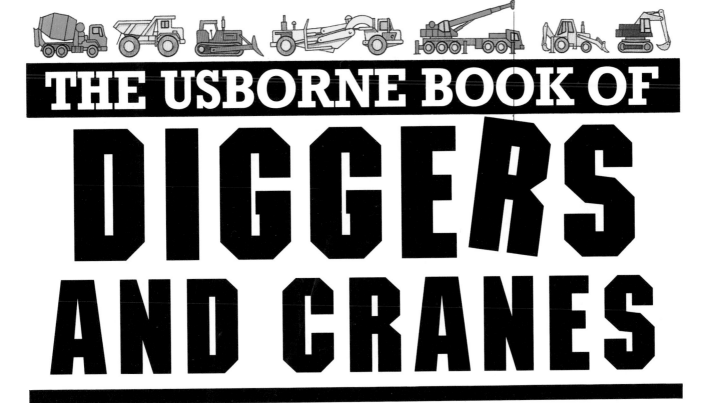

THE USBORNE BOOK OF DIGGERS AND CRANES

Consultant: D. Wheeler (Senior Plant Engineer, George Wimpey Ltd.)

Contents

 # Bulldozers

Bulldozers clear the ground ready for building. They push earth, stones and tree stumps out of their way with a huge metal blade. This is called dozing.

Crawler tracks

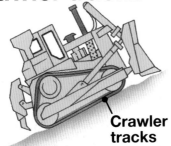

Crawler tracks

Crawler tracks help the heavy bulldozer climb up steep banks.

They can go over bumps more smoothly than wheels, too.

They help stop the bulldozer sinking into soft, muddy ground.

This is where the driver sits. It is called a cab.

The cab has a frame of metal bars. They protect the driver if the bulldozer rolls over.

This bulldozer has a powerful engine. It can push things much heavier than itself.

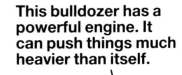

In hot countries, the cab has no glass in its windows. This keeps the driver cool.

Fire extinguisher

This tool is called a ripper. It drags behind the bulldozer breaking up hard, stony ground.

Metal crawler tracks cover the bulldozer's wheels.

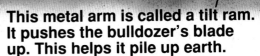

This metal arm is called a tilt ram. It pushes the bulldozer's blade up. This helps it pile up earth.

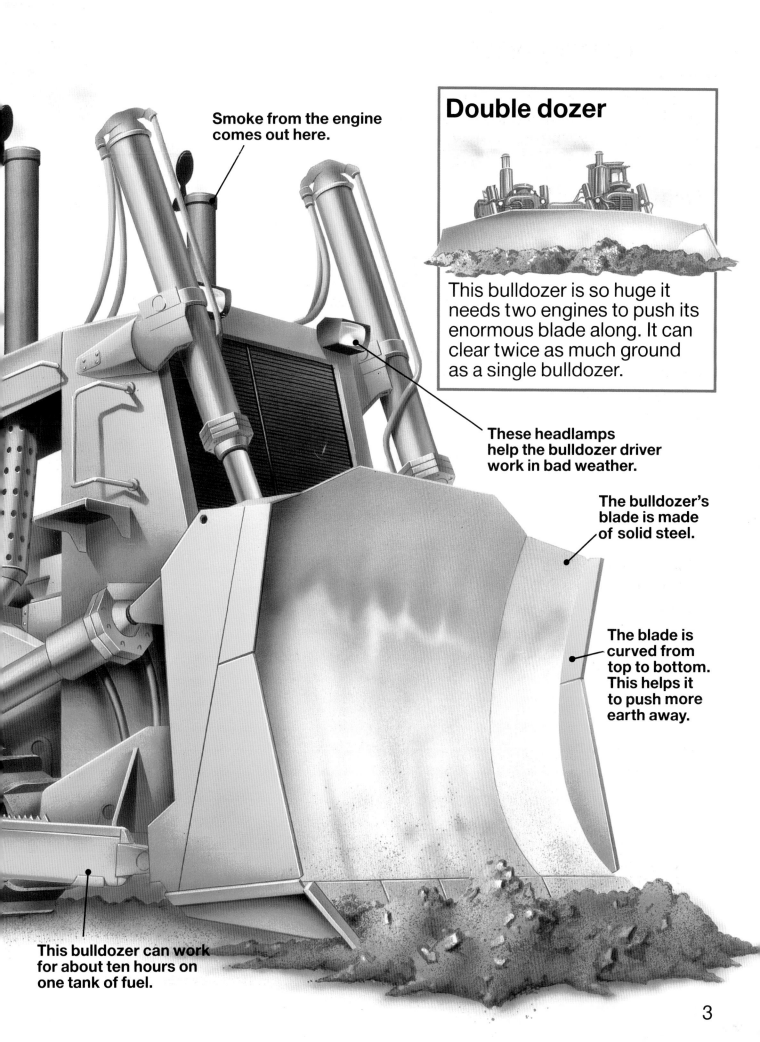

Smoke from the engine comes out here.

Double dozer

This bulldozer is so huge it needs two engines to push its enormous blade along. It can clear twice as much ground as a single bulldozer.

These headlamps help the bulldozer driver work in bad weather.

The bulldozer's blade is made of solid steel.

The blade is curved from top to bottom. This helps it to push more earth away.

This bulldozer can work for about ten hours on one tank of fuel.

3

Backhoe excavator

Digging machines are called excavators. There are lots of different sorts. Excavators can do other jobs, too. You can see some at work at the bottom of this page.

This digger is a backhoe excavator. It digs into the ground with a metal bucket called a backhoe.

These are rams. They slide in and out of their metal case. This makes the excavator's arm move.

This bucket can dig up more than 500 spadefuls of earth at a time.

This is the dipper arm. It dips in and out of the ground as the excavator digs.

These metal teeth cut through the earth easily.

This is the boom. The driver can make it shorter or longer for each digging job.

This mini-excavator is so small it could fit into the backhoe excavator's bucket. It does small digging jobs.

Other excavators

These excavators have tools that do many different jobs.

This excavator can carry earth in a loader bucket.

Claws help this excavator pick up pipes or logs.

This excavator's metal grab picks things up easily.

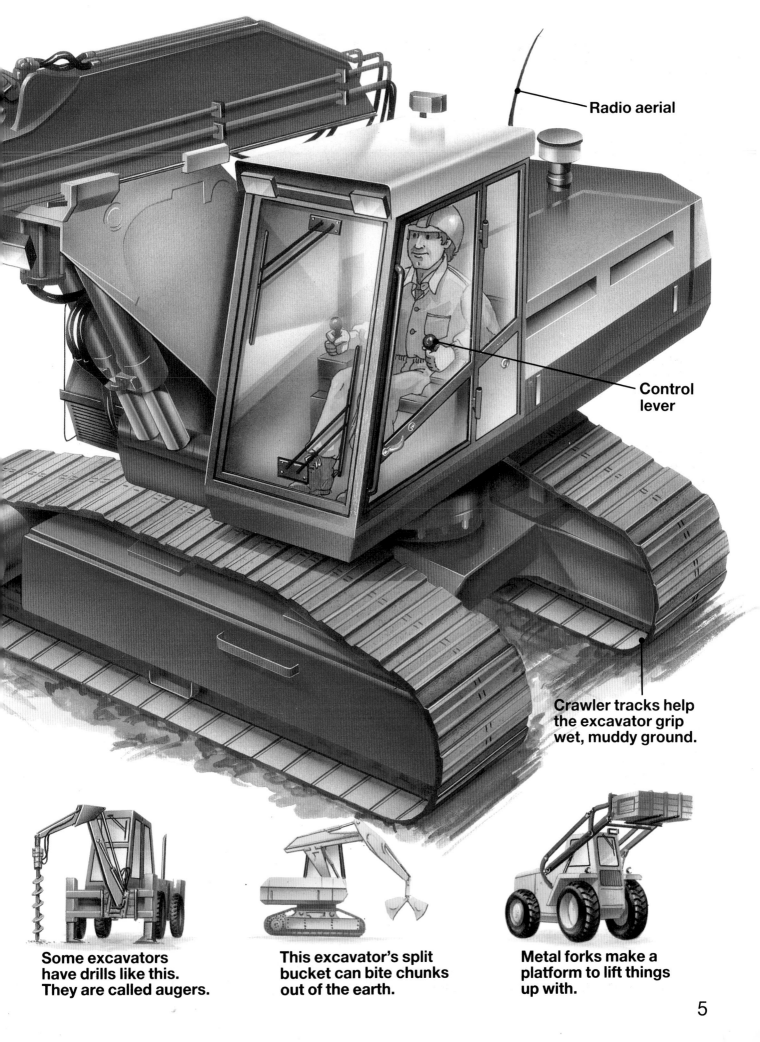

Radio aerial

Control
lever

Crawler tracks help
the excavator grip
wet, muddy ground.

Some excavators
have drills like this.
They are called augers.

This excavator's split
bucket can bite chunks
out of the earth.

Metal forks make a
platform to lift things
up with.

Backhoe loader

This excavator can do many digging jobs. It can dig pits and trenches with a backhoe or scoop up earth in a bucket called a loader. It is called a backhoe loader.

The cab has glass all the way round. The driver has a good view as he controls the machine.

The driver can turn his seat to face the loader or the backhoe.

Headlight

This bucket is called the backhoe.

The driver uses these two levers to control the backhoe.

Up and down

Backhoe

The backhoe can stretch up as high as an upstairs window to dig.

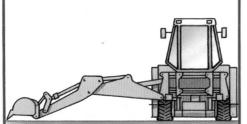

It can swivel around and dig at the side of the excavator, like this.

It can also reach down like this to scoop up earth and dig a trench.

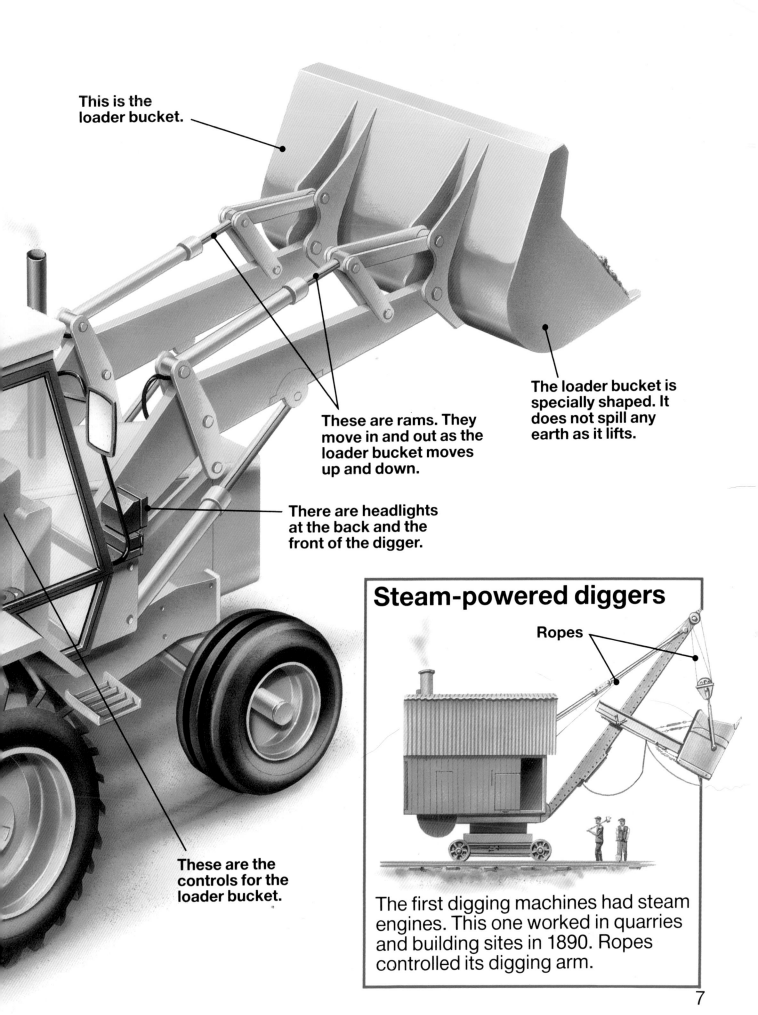

This is the loader bucket.

These are rams. They move in and out as the loader bucket moves up and down.

The loader bucket is specially shaped. It does not spill any earth as it lifts.

There are headlights at the back and the front of the digger.

These are the controls for the loader bucket.

Steam-powered diggers

Ropes

The first digging machines had steam engines. This one worked in quarries and building sites in 1890. Ropes controlled its digging arm.

7

Moving cranes

These cranes move around on wheels or crawler tracks. They are called truck cranes and crawler cranes. They can move quickly from job to job.

The arm a crane lifts with is called a jib or a boom.

This boom has four parts. They fold away inside each other like this when the crane is not lifting.

Ready to lift

Boom

The truck crane arrives at the building site with its boom folded up.

Outrigger

Metal legs called outriggers lift the crane off the ground.

The boom slowly lifts up and slides out ready to lift a load.

Truck crane

Truck cranes are built on the back of a truck.

When it slides out, this boom can stretch up to the top of a six floor building.

A truck crane has two cabs. One is for driving the truck. The other is to control the crane.

Crane cab

The crane's engine is under here.

This is an outrigger. It supports the crane while it is lifting.

Outriggers slide away underneath the truck crane when it is not lifting.

The crane's wheels are not touching the ground.

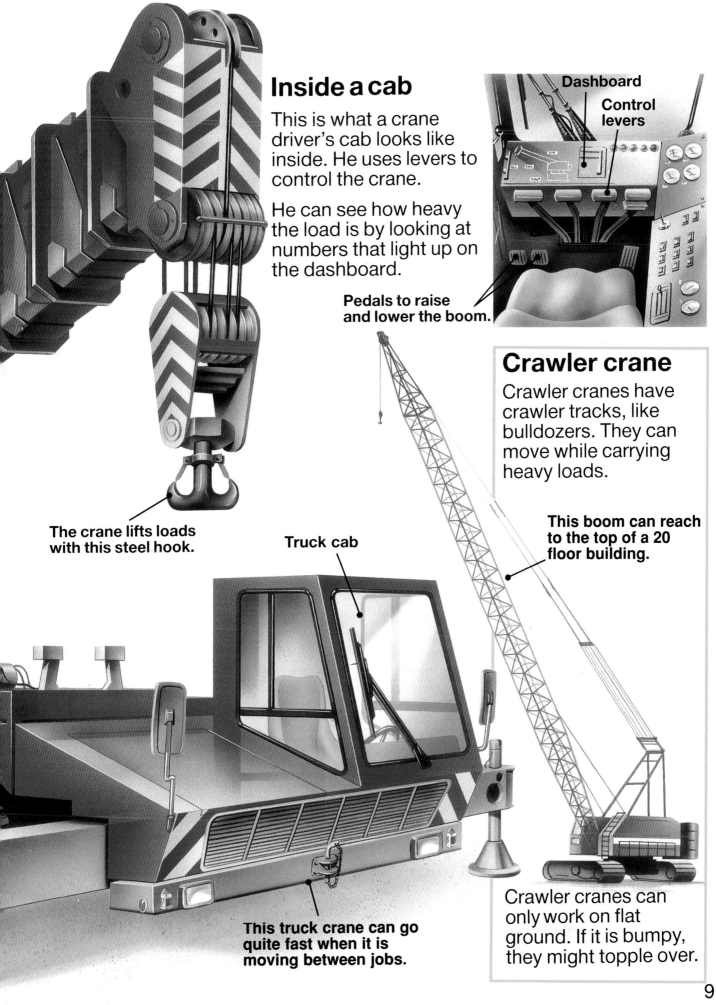

Inside a cab

This is what a crane driver's cab looks like inside. He uses levers to control the crane.

He can see how heavy the load is by looking at numbers that light up on the dashboard.

Dashboard

Control levers

Pedals to raise and lower the boom.

The crane lifts loads with this steel hook.

Truck cab

Crawler crane

Crawler cranes have crawler tracks, like bulldozers. They can move while carrying heavy loads.

This boom can reach to the top of a 20 floor building.

This truck crane can go quite fast when it is moving between jobs.

Crawler cranes can only work on flat ground. If it is bumpy, they might topple over.

Tower cranes

The biggest cranes in the world are called tower cranes. They are put up bit by bit on the building site. Tower cranes help build tall buildings such as skyscrapers.

Trolley tower crane

This is a trolley tower crane. It has a trolley running up and down a long arm called a jib. The load hangs from the trolley on ropes.

This is a latticed jib. The criss-crossed metal pattern is called latticing. It is lighter than solid metal.

Drum

Trolley

Hoist ropes

This is the driver's cab. He may have to climb over 100 steps to reach it.

This is a winch. As it turns around, it winds ropes around a drum. This moves the crane's hook up and down.

These blocks of concrete are called the counterweight. Their weight stops the crane toppling over when it lifts heavy loads.

The crane lifts its load with this metal hook.

Ladder

This tower crane can swing around in a complete circle.

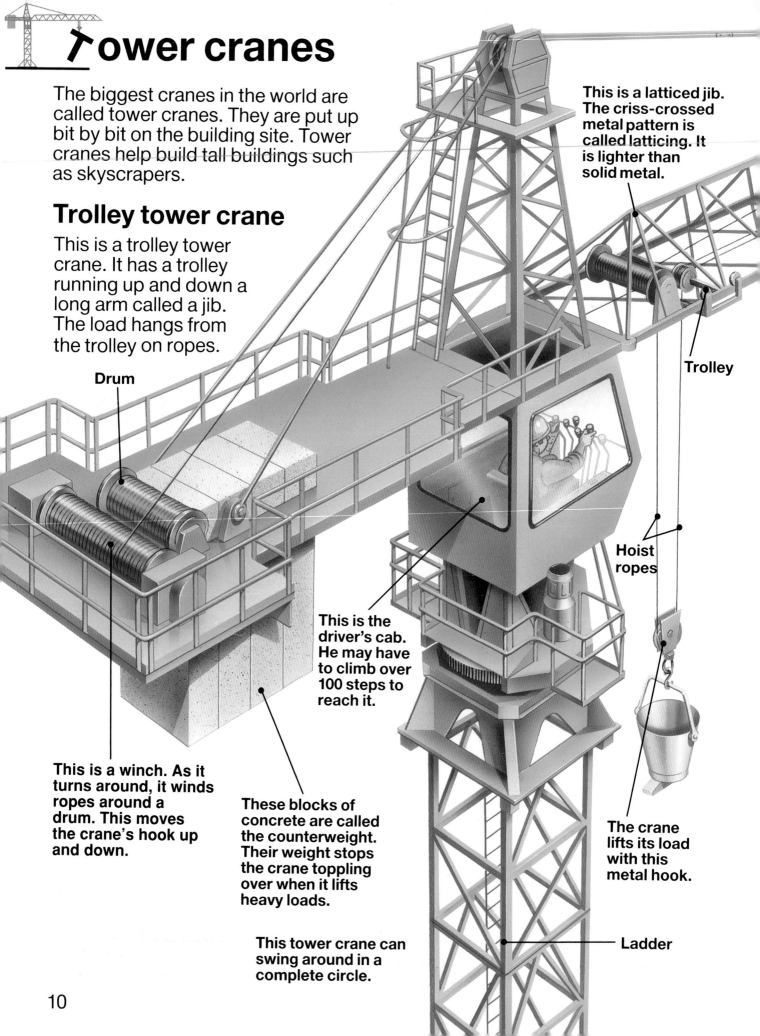

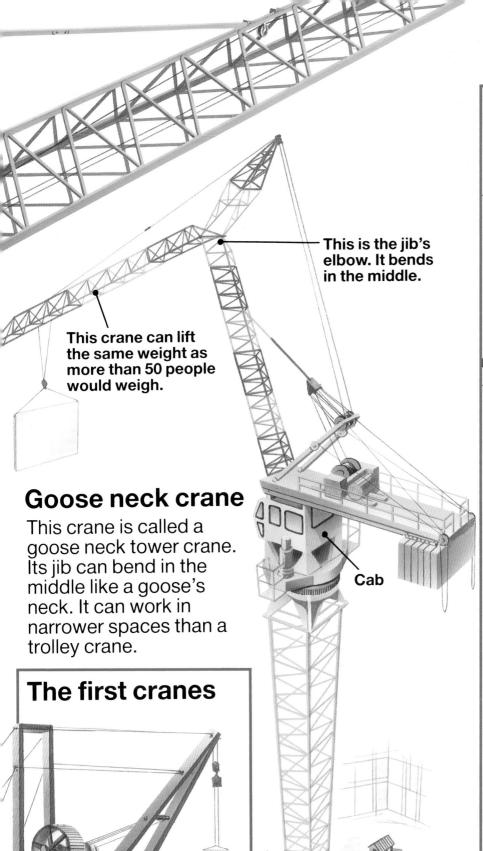

This is the jib's elbow. It bends in the middle.

This crane can lift the same weight as more than 50 people would weigh.

Goose neck crane

This crane is called a goose neck tower crane. Its jib can bend in the middle like a goose's neck. It can work in narrower spaces than a trolley crane.

Cab

The first cranes

The Romans built the first cranes. Slaves ran around inside a wooden wheel with ropes tied to it. This lifted things up.

The crane rests on heavy metal rails. Concrete blocks hold it in place.

Bit by bit

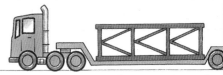

Trucks bring the parts of the tower crane to the building site.

A truck crane lifts the pieces of the tower crane into place.

Builders bolt the bits of the crane's jib together on the ground.

Jib

Cab

The cab and the jib are lifted into place by the truck crane.

Counterweight

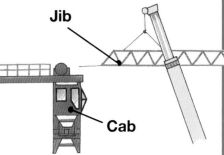

The truck crane lifts the counterweight. Now the crane is ready to work.

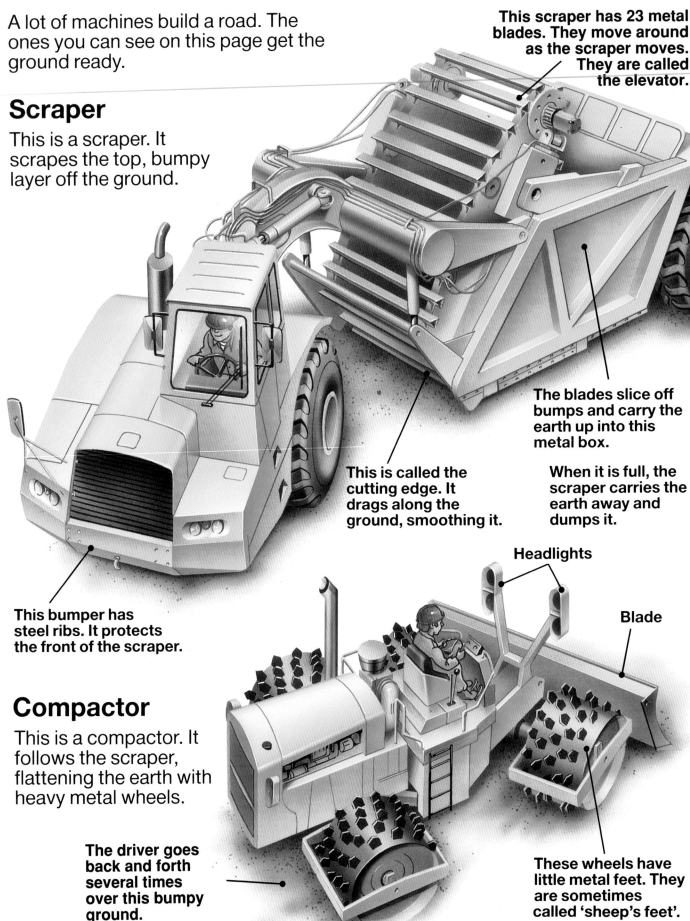

Building roads 1

A lot of machines build a road. The ones you can see on this page get the ground ready.

Scraper

This is a scraper. It scrapes the top, bumpy layer off the ground.

This scraper has 23 metal blades. They move around as the scraper moves. They are called the elevator.

The blades slice off bumps and carry the earth up into this metal box.

When it is full, the scraper carries the earth away and dumps it.

This is called the cutting edge. It drags along the ground, smoothing it.

This bumper has steel ribs. It protects the front of the scraper.

Headlights

Blade

Compactor

This is a compactor. It follows the scraper, flattening the earth with heavy metal wheels.

The driver goes back and forth several times over this bumpy ground.

These wheels have little metal feet. They are sometimes called 'sheep's feet'.

12

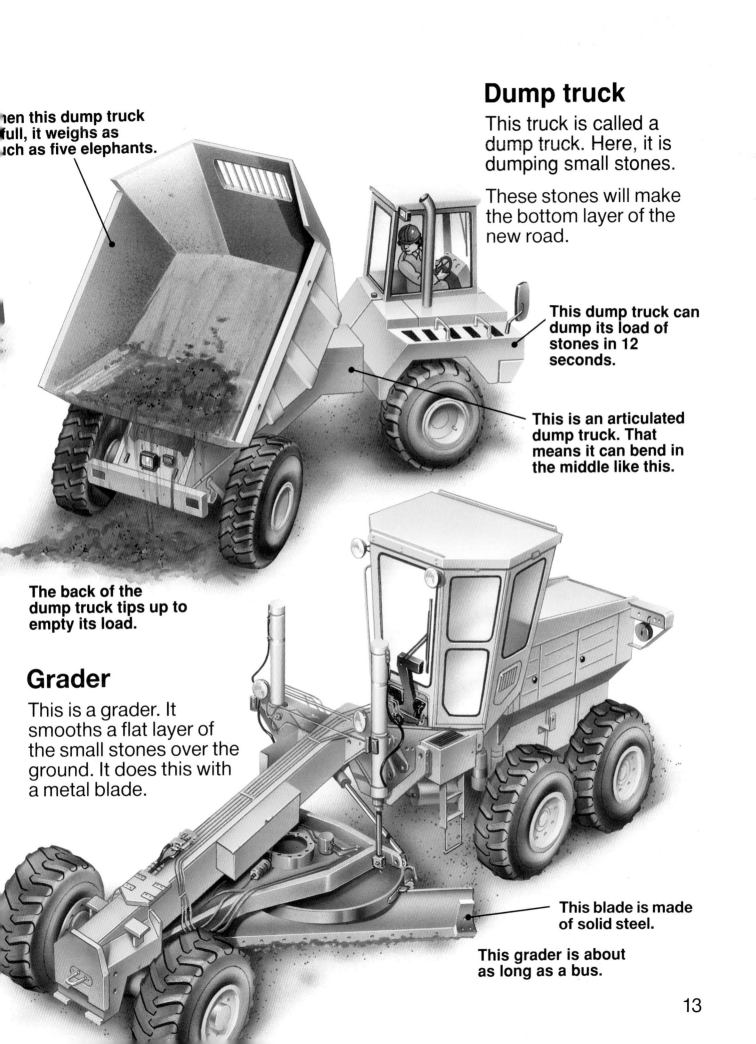

When this dump truck full, it weighs as much as five elephants.

Dump truck

This truck is called a dump truck. Here, it is dumping small stones.

These stones will make the bottom layer of the new road.

This dump truck can dump its load of stones in 12 seconds.

This is an articulated dump truck. That means it can bend in the middle like this.

The back of the dump truck tips up to empty its load.

Grader

This is a grader. It smooths a flat layer of the small stones over the ground. It does this with a metal blade.

This blade is made of solid steel.

This grader is about as long as a bus.

Building roads 2

A paver lays a mixture of hot tar and small stones on the road. A roller makes sure the road is flat.

Roller

This roller drives slowly behind the paver. It flattens the tar and stones with its heavy metal rollers.

It will go over the road several times to make it ready for cars and trucks to drive on it.

Steam rollers

The first rollers were called steam rollers. They had engines powered by steam. This steam roller was built in about 1847. It went very slowly.

This roller weighs about as much as 18 cars.

This builder is checking that the edge of the new road is neat.

There are small water sprinklers above each roller. They keep them clean and cool.

These wheels are hollow. They can be filled with water or sand. This makes the roller even heavier.

Paver

A mixture of hot tar and small stones is called asphalt. A paver spreads a layer of warm asphalt over the road. It sets hard as it cools.

Filling up

A truck tips asphalt into a box called a hopper. It is at the front of the paver.

The asphalt goes through the paver and comes out of the back as it moves.

The truck can fill the paver with asphalt while it works.

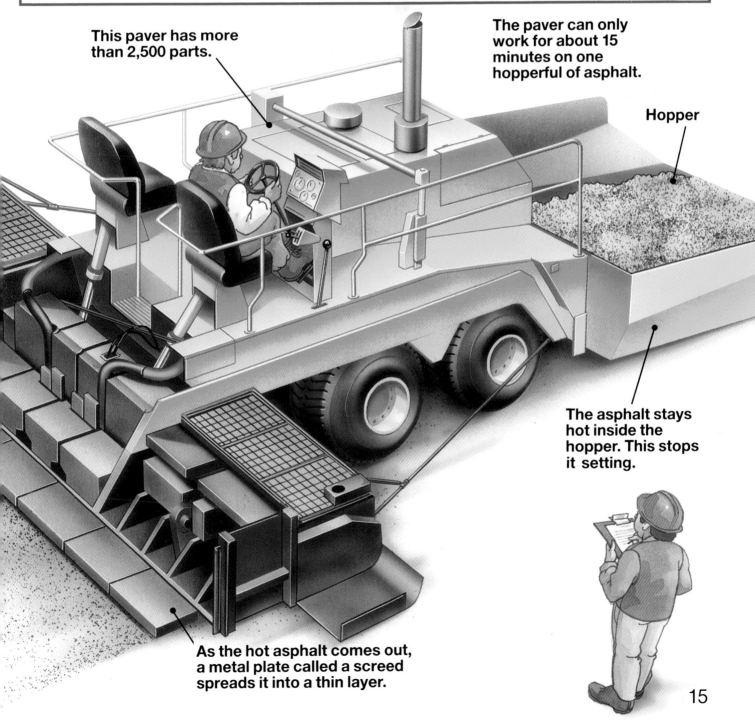

This paver has more than 2,500 parts.

The paver can only work for about 15 minutes on one hopperful of asphalt.

Hopper

The asphalt stays hot inside the hopper. This stops it setting.

As the hot asphalt comes out, a metal plate called a screed spreads it into a thin layer.

15

At the docks

Lots of different cranes work at the docks. Some are specially built to lift loads on and off ships. Others move cargo from place to place.

Container cranes

Many cargoes come in metal boxes, or containers. Cranes called container cranes can pick them up.

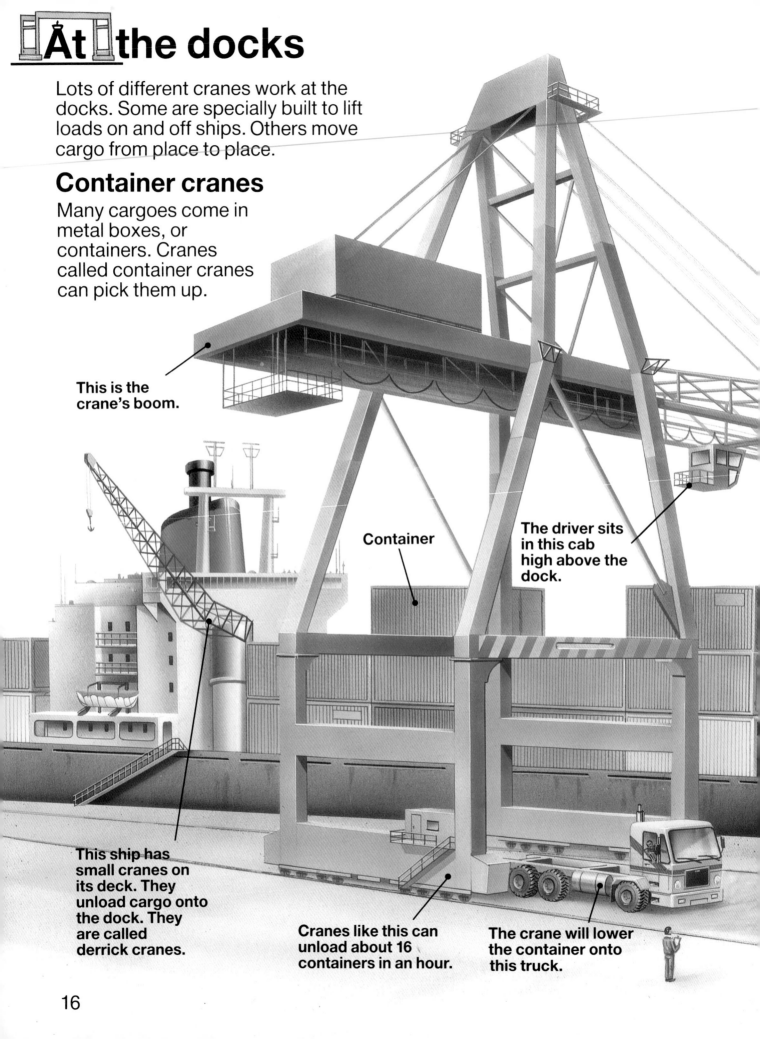

This is the crane's boom.

Container

The driver sits in this cab high above the dock.

This ship has small cranes on its deck. They unload cargo onto the dock. They are called derrick cranes.

Cranes like this can unload about 16 containers in an hour.

The crane will lower the container onto this truck.

Carrying containers

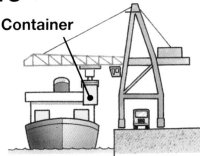

Boom

Trolley

Container

The crane's boom is above the ship. Ropes and clamps hang down from a trolley.

The clamps grab the edges of the container. The driver pulls a lever and ropes lift it up.

The trolley slides back along the boom. The ropes slowly lower the container onto a truck.

Several container cranes work side by side at big docks.

Each of these containers is taller than two people standing on each others' shoulders.

Straddle Carrier

This crane is called a straddle carrier. It picks up containers and drives them away to stack them up.

This crane can stack four containers on top of each other.

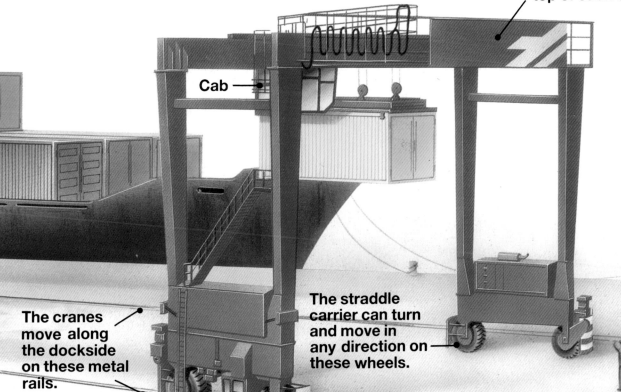

Cab

The cranes move along the dockside on these metal rails.

The straddle carrier can turn and move in any direction on these wheels.

 # Building machines

Tall buildings are very heavy. The ground must be strong to hold them up. These machines are drilling holes in the ground and filling them with concrete and steel rods. This will strengthen the ground.

Underground legs

Auger

First a crane drills a hole in the ground with a tool called an auger. It is fixed to the crane's jib.

Then a mobile crane lowers long steel rods down into each hole. They make steel 'legs'.

Concrete comes out here.

A concrete pump fills the holes with concrete. Now the ground is strong enough to build on.

Concrete mixer

The hollow drum on the back of a concrete mixer can turn around. It has metal blades inside it to mix concrete.

The drum turns around about eight times a minute to mix concrete.

The chalk, stones and sand to make concrete are poured in here.

Water to make concrete is in this tank.

The builder controls the mixer's drum with levers.

Concrete pours out of this metal tube.

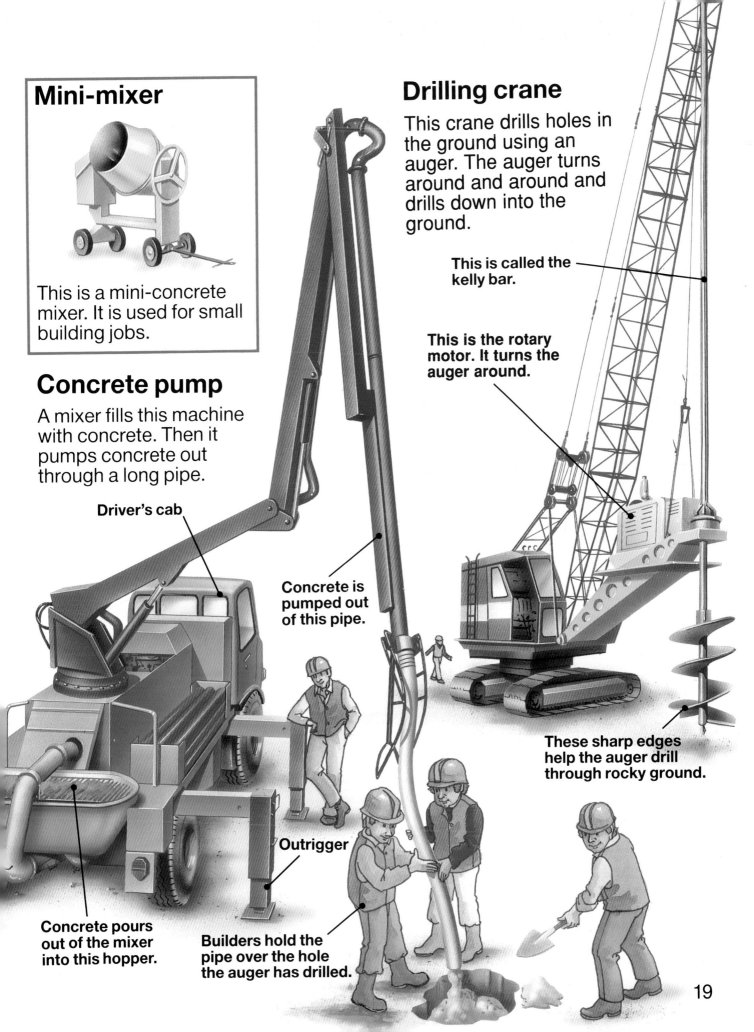

Mini-mixer

This is a mini-concrete mixer. It is used for small building jobs.

Concrete pump

A mixer fills this machine with concrete. Then it pumps concrete out through a long pipe.

Driver's cab

Concrete is pumped out of this pipe.

Concrete pours out of the mixer into this hopper.

Outrigger

Builders hold the pipe over the hole the auger has drilled.

Drilling crane

This crane drills holes in the ground using an auger. The auger turns around and around and drills down into the ground.

This is called the kelly bar.

This is the rotary motor. It turns the auger around.

These sharp edges help the auger drill through rocky ground.

19

Mining machines

Here are some of the diggers that work in mines. They dig up valuable things like coal, copper and gold. Some work underground and others dig on the earth's surface.

Bucket wheel excavator

Sometimes, coal is buried only just under the ground. This huge machine digs it up. It is called a bucket wheel excavator.

These wires lower the wheel until it is touching the ground.

Boom

The wheel turns around and around.

Buckets scrape up the coal as the wheel turns.

This sharp edge bites into the ground.

This excavator has 18 buckets. Each one can hold enough to fill a car with coal.

The wheel can scrape up about 40,000 bucketsful of coal in one day.

When all the coal is gone, people sometimes cover the mine with earth and plant grass again.

The driver sits in this cab to control the huge machine.

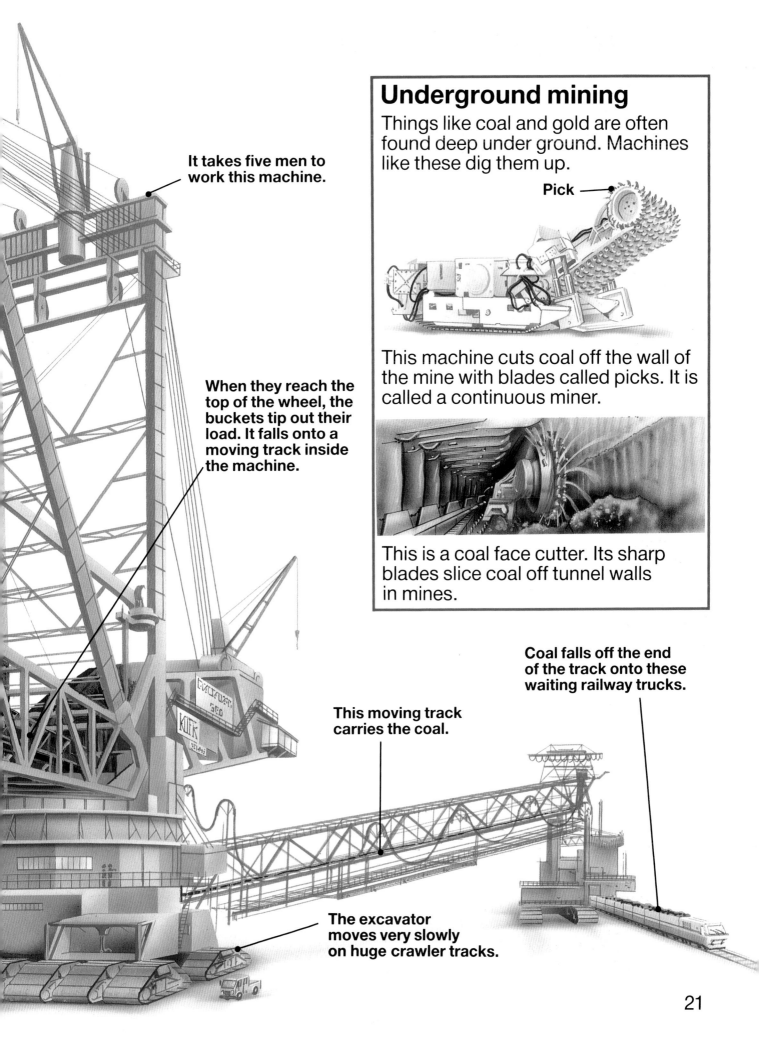

It takes five men to work this machine.

Underground mining

Things like coal and gold are often found deep under ground. Machines like these dig them up.

Pick

This machine cuts coal off the wall of the mine with blades called picks. It is called a continuous miner.

This is a coal face cutter. Its sharp blades slice coal off tunnel walls in mines.

When they reach the top of the wheel, the buckets tip out their load. It falls onto a moving track inside the machine.

Coal falls off the end of the track onto these waiting railway trucks.

This moving track carries the coal.

The excavator moves very slowly on huge crawler tracks.

21

Diggers and drills

People dig up stones and rock in quarries to use for building. They use these powerful machines.

Dragline excavator

This machine is called a dragline excavator. It can dig up much more than any other excavator in its huge steel bucket.

Boom

Dragging the bucket

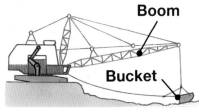

Boom

Bucket

The excavator has a bucket on the end of its boom. It lowers it onto the ground in front of it.

Dragline

Wires called draglines drag the bucket towards the excavator. It fills up with earth and rock.

When the bucket is full, the excavator empties it. Then the draglines let the bucket go again.

This bucket is big enough for a car to park inside it.

Dragline

Face shovel

A wall of solid rock is called a rock face. This machine digs into it. It is called a face shovel.

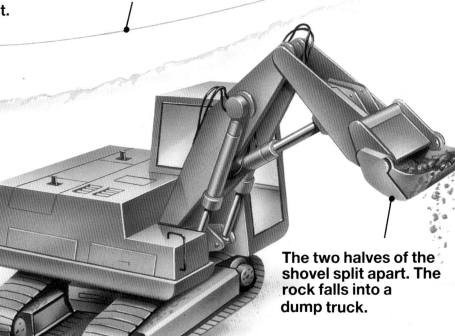

The two halves of the shovel split apart. The rock falls into a dump truck.

Crawler tracks hold the face shovel steady as it digs.

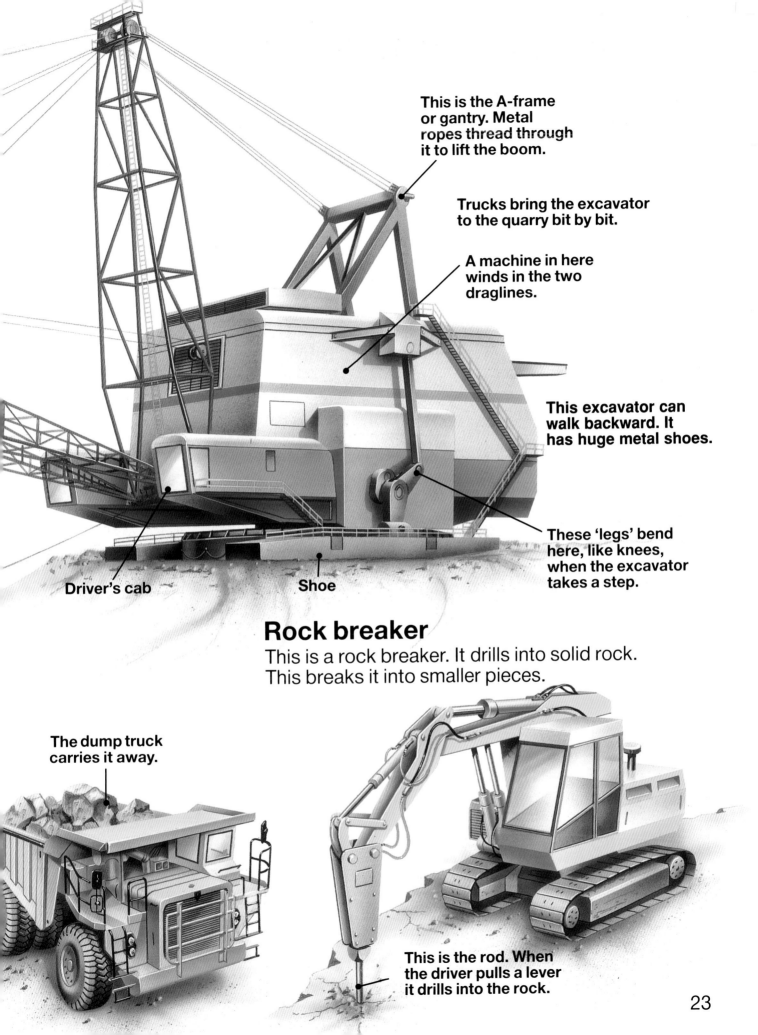

This is the A-frame or gantry. Metal ropes thread through it to lift the boom.

Trucks bring the excavator to the quarry bit by bit.

A machine in here winds in the two draglines.

This excavator can walk backward. It has huge metal shoes.

These 'legs' bend here, like knees, when the excavator takes a step.

Driver's cab

Shoe

Rock breaker

This is a rock breaker. It drills into solid rock. This breaks it into smaller pieces.

The dump truck carries it away.

This is the rod. When the driver pulls a lever it drills into the rock.

23

Floating diggers and cranes

The machines you can see here work out at sea, or on rivers. They are built on top of a boat.

Giant crane

This is a giant floating crane. It works at sea, sailing from job to job. About 350 men live and work on it.

There is a cinema, restaurant and a hospital on board the crane.

Two huge cranes and a smaller crawler crane work on the giant crane.

These are the crane's booms. They are so strong, they can lift whole ships.

The deck of this crane is as long as three swimming pools put end to end.

This is a helipad. Helicopters land on and take off from it.

This hook is about twice as tall as a person.

The crane has two huge propellers under the deck. They push it slowly through the water.

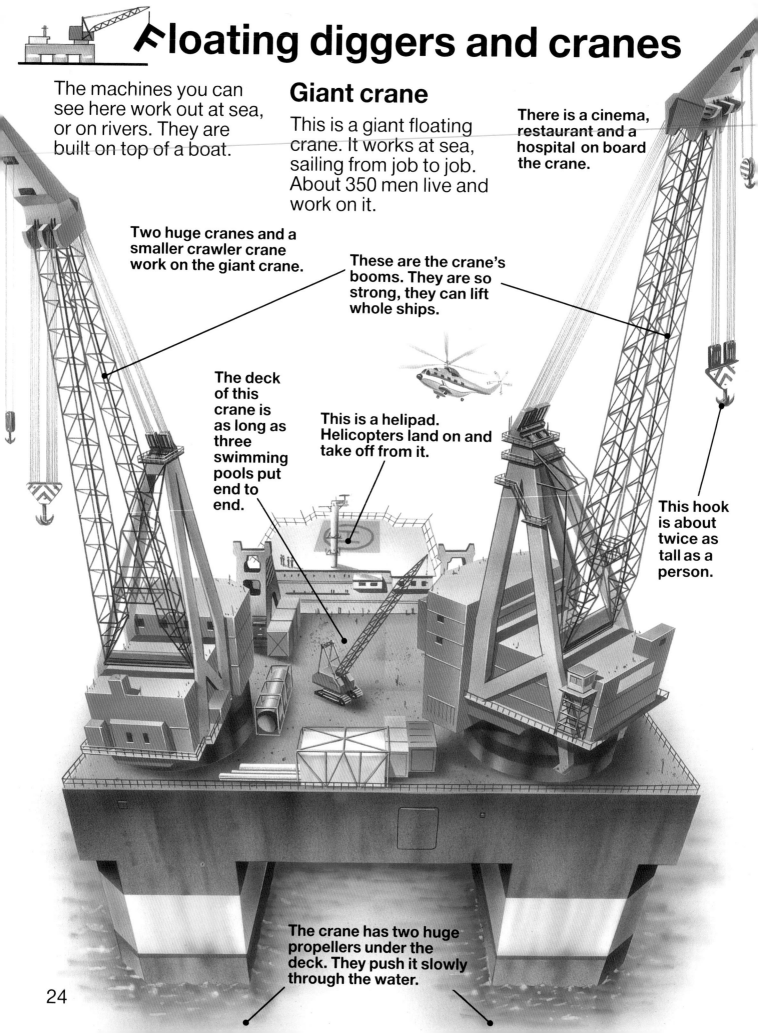

Dredgers

Dredgers dig up mud and sand from the bottom of seas and rivers. This one is called a bucket dredger. It digs up mud in a chain of buckets called a ladder. They go around and around like a moving staircase.

How a dredger works

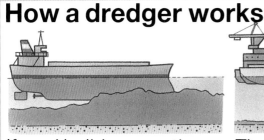

If mud builds up on the sea bed or a river bed, ships can get stuck on it.

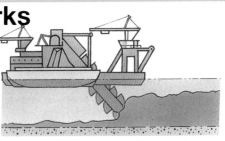

The dredger scoops the mud from the bottom and dumps it on barges.

The barges carry it out to sea. They dump it where the water is deep.

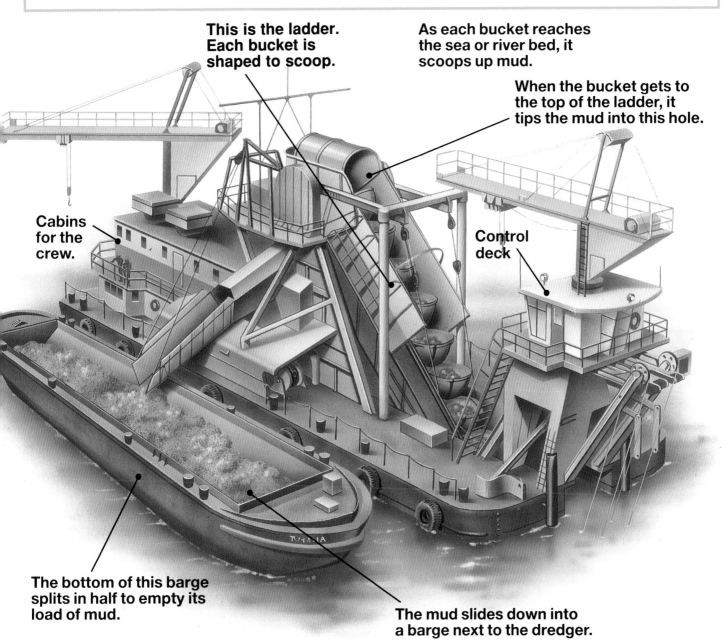

This is the ladder. Each bucket is shaped to scoop.

As each bucket reaches the sea or river bed, it scoops up mud.

When the bucket gets to the top of the ladder, it tips the mud into this hole.

Cabins for the crew.

Control deck

The bottom of this barge splits in half to empty its load of mud.

The mud slides down into a barge next to the dredger.

Tunnel diggers

Tunnelling machines have to be able to dig through earth, mud and even solid rock. The biggest tunnelling machines in the world are called TBMs. This stands for Tunnel Boring Machine.

Early tunnels

Builders covered the inside of the tunnel with bricks behind the machine.

This metal cage protected the men from falling earth.

This is one of the first tunnelling machines. It dug tunnels for underground trains in London over 170 years ago. Builders dug through earth with spades at the front as the machine moved forward.

A TBM

Tunnel Boring Machines like this one dug the Channel Tunnel under the sea between England and France. Here you can see what part of a TBM looks like inside.

The TBM grips the inside of the tunnel with four metal plates like these. They are called gripper shoes.

This is a segment erector. It covers the inside of the tunnel with concrete segments .

Cutterhead

The dug-out earth from the cutterhead is carried out on this moving belt.

The TBM has 20 rams like this. They push it forward as it digs.

This is the cutterhead. It spins around and cuts through the earth with sharp blades.

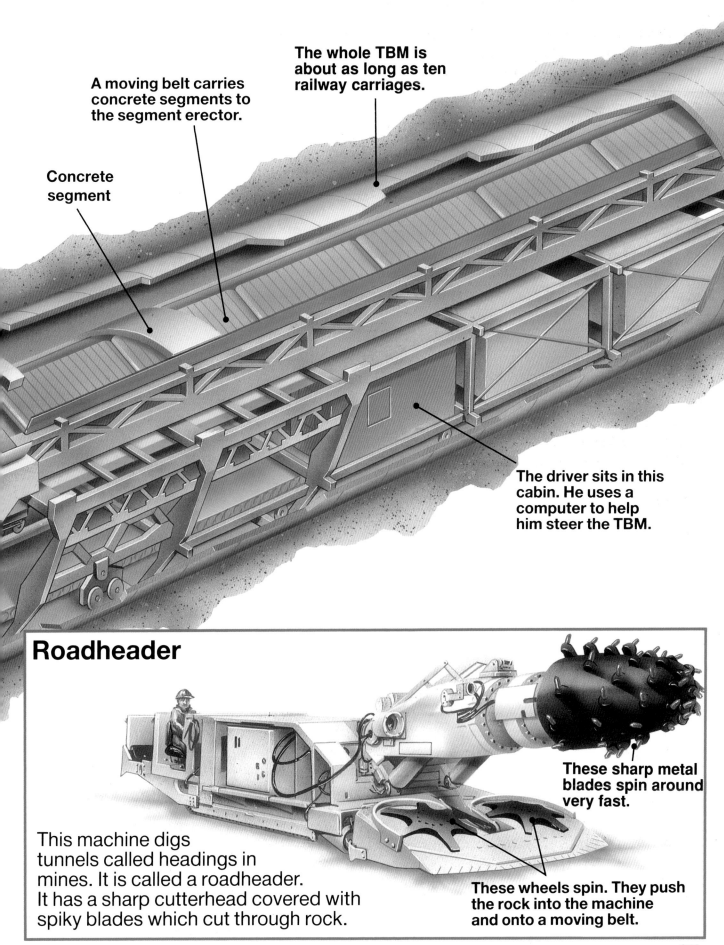

A moving belt carries concrete segments to the segment erector.

The whole TBM is about as long as ten railway carriages.

Concrete segment

The driver sits in this cabin. He uses a computer to help him steer the TBM.

Roadheader

This machine digs tunnels called headings in mines. It is called a roadheader. It has a sharp cutterhead covered with spiky blades which cut through rock.

These sharp metal blades spin around very fast.

These wheels spin. They push the rock into the machine and onto a moving belt.

Machine facts 1

On the next four pages are some facts about many of the machines in this book. They are medium-sized examples of each machine.

Bulldozer

Height: 3.5 m/11.5 ft
Length: 6.3 m/21 ft
Fastest speed: 10.5 kph/ 6.3 mph

Backhoe excavator

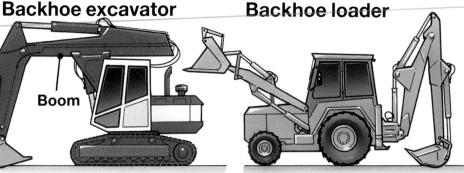

Boom

Height: 4 m/13 ft
Length: 3.5 m/11.5 ft
Length of boom: 2.4 m/ 8.5 ft

Backhoe loader

Height: 3 m/10 ft
Length: 6.18 m/20.5 ft
Deepest dig: 4.3 m/14 ft

Excavator with claws

Claws

Height: 3 m/10 ft
Length: 6.2 m/25.5 ft
Number of claws: 2

Excavator with grab

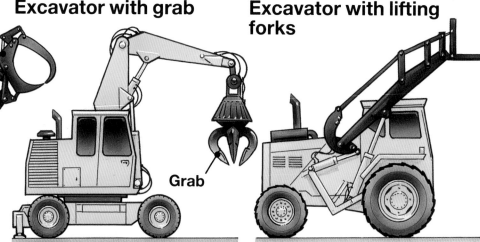

Grab

Height: 3.2 m/10.5 ft
Length: 4.6 m/15 ft
Number of fingers: 5

Excavator with lifting forks

Height: 3 m/10 ft
Length: 6.2 m/20.5 ft
Highest stretch: 3.5 m/ 11.5 ft

Loader excavator

Height: 3.5 m/11.5 ft
Length: 7.3 m/24 ft
Bucket load: 10,360 kg/ 22,839 lbs

Scraper

Blade

Height: 3.3 m/11 ft
Length: 10 m/30 ft
Number of blades: 23

Compactor

Height: 3.5 m/11.5 ft
Length: 6.8 m/22.5 ft
Weight: 20 tonnes/ 19.6 tons

Grader

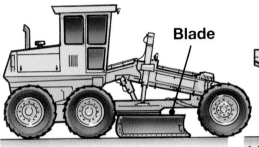

Blade

Height: 3.3 m/11 ft
Length: 7 m/23 ft
Length of blade: 4.2 m/
15 ft

Articulated dump truck

Height: 2.8 m/9 ft
Length: 6.5 m/21.5 ft
Biggest load: 12 tonnes/
11.8 tons

Heavy load dump truck

Height: 4 m/13 ft
Length: 9 m/30 ft
Biggest load: 55 tonnes/
54 tons

Roller

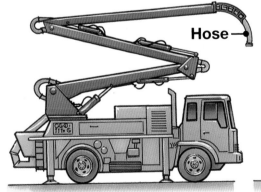

Height: 3 m/10 ft
Length: 5.2 m/18 ft
Biggest load: 10 tonnes/
9.8 tons

Paver

Height: 3 m/10 ft
Length: 5.9 m/19.5 ft
Fastest speed: 15 kph/
9.3 mph

Concrete mixer

Drum

Height: 3.5 m/11.5 ft
Length: 5.9 m/19.5 ft
Drum speed: 12 turns per
minute

Concrete pump

Hose

Height: 3 m/10 ft
Length: 8 m/26.5 ft
Full length of hose: 23 m/
76 ft

Rock breaker

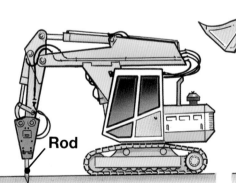

Rod

Height: 3.4 m/11 ft
Length of tracks: 3 m/10 ft
Length of rod: 0.6 m/2 ft

Power shovel

Height: 4.5 m/15 ft
Length: 6.3 m/21 ft
Highest stretch: 10 m/33 ft

Machine facts 2

Dragline excavator

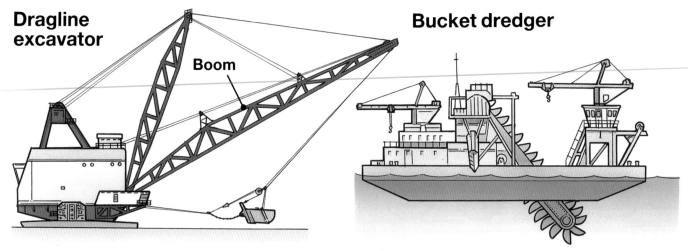

Boom

Height: 50 m/165 ft
Boom length: 79 m/261 ft
Crew: 2 people

Bucket dredger

Height: 23 m/76 ft
Length: 58 m/192 ft
Deepest dig: 25 m/83 ft

TBM (Tunnel Boring Machine)

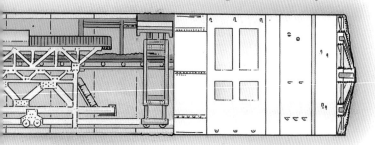

Height: 8.36 m/27.5 ft
Length: 220 m/726 ft
Digging speed: 6 m per
hour/20 ft per hour

Roadheader

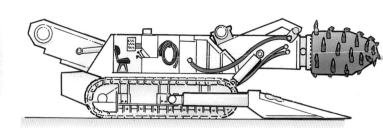

Height: 10 m/33 ft
Length: 9 m/30 ft
Weight: 42 tonnes/
41.3 tons

Continuous miner

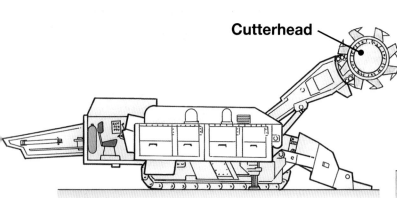

Cutterhead

Height: 1.5 m/5 ft
Length: 10.6 m/35 ft
Speed of cutterhead: 50
turns per minute

Bucket wheel excavator

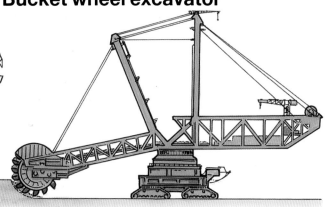

Number of buckets: 10
Deepest dig: 50 m/165 ft
Crew: 2 people

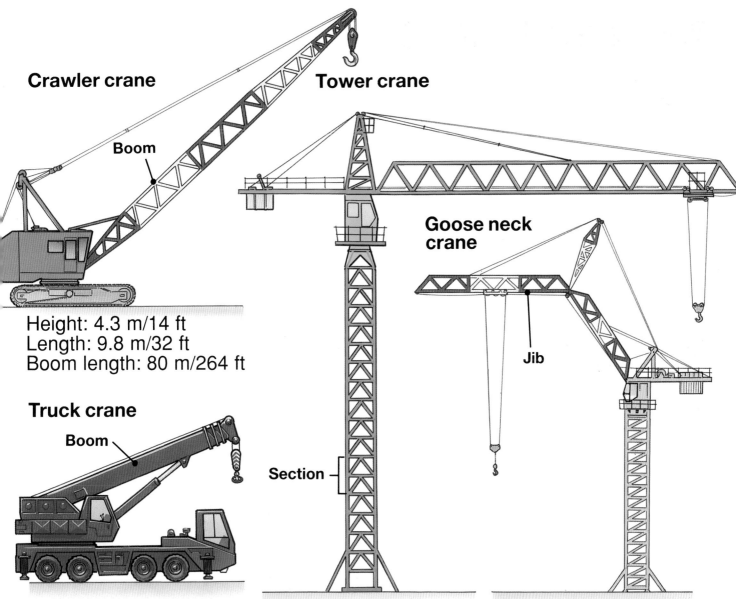

Crawler crane

Boom

Height: 4.3 m/14 ft
Length: 9.8 m/32 ft
Boom length: 80 m/264 ft

Truck crane

Boom

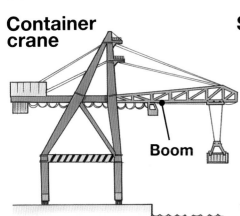

Height: 3.8 m/12.5 ft
Length: 12 m/39.5 ft
Longest boom length:
35 m/ 116 ft

Tower crane

Section

Height: 65 m/215 ft
Section height: 6 m/20 ft
Biggest load: 20 tonnes/
19.6 tons

Goose neck crane

Jib

Height: 104 m/334 ft
Jib length: 34 m/112 ft
Biggest load: 12 tonnes/
11.8 tons

Container crane

Boom

Height: 60 m/198 ft
Boom length: 80 m/264 ft
Biggest load: 50 tonnes/
49.2 tons

Straddle carrier

Boom

Height: 12 m/39.5 ft
Boom length: 12 m/39.5 ft
Biggest load: 50 tonnes/
49.2 tons

Giant floating crane

Boom

Length: 154 m/508 ft
Biggest load:
1,000 tonnes/984 tons
Number of booms: 2

Picture puzzle

Here are parts of some of the machines that are in this section of the book. Can you remember which machines they belong to and what they are called?

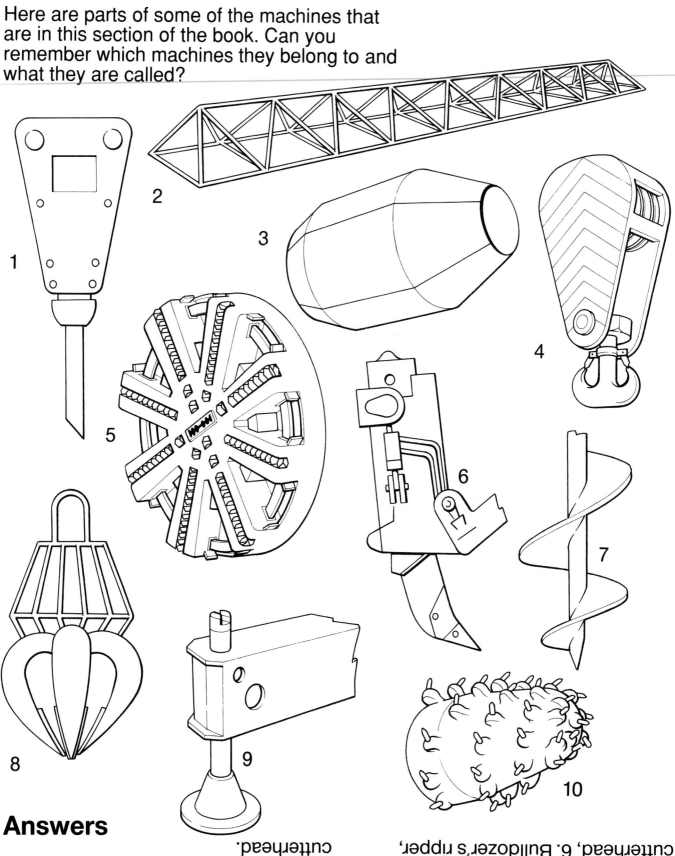

Answers

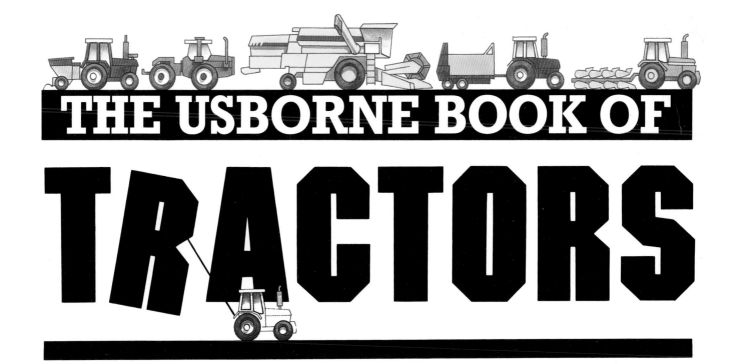

THE USBORNE BOOK OF TRACTORS

Consultant: Mick Roberts (Machinery Editor, Farmers Weekly)

Contents

Tractor

Tractors have to do many different jobs on a farm and can work in all sorts of weather.

Farmers drive them over bumpy, muddy fields, so they have to be tough and hard-wearing.

This is the tractor's cab, where the driver sits.

This is the tractor's engine. It is powerful, but does not use much fuel.

Tractors can go on roads but they cannot move as fast as cars or trucks.

When these lights are switched on, the tractor can even work at night.

Tractors need tough, thick tyres.

The main part of the tractor is called the chassis.

Tractor tyres have deep grooves in them. They grip wet, muddy ground without getting stuck.

A tractor's body is high above the wheels. This stops it getting damaged by rocky, bumpy ground.

Its powerful engine keeps the tractor going up any sloping ground around the farm, too.

This light flashes when the tractor drives on roads. Other drivers see it and slow down.

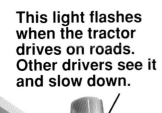

This back window opens to let fresh air into the cab in hot weather.

The cab has a heater for cold weather.

Tractors can tip right over if they drive up very steep slopes. These metal bars stop the farmer getting crushed if that happens.

Tractors can turn around in small spaces. They must not squash crops in the fields.

Three links

Tractors pull many different farming tools behind them.

The tools are fixed to three metal links behind the cab. A metal pole called a Power Take-Off (P.T.O.) carries power from the tractor's engine to the tools. This makes them work.

P.T.O.

Three links

 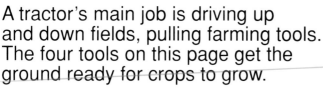 # Tractors at work

A tractor's main job is driving up and down fields, pulling farming tools. The four tools on this page get the ground ready for crops to grow.

Plough

This tractor is pulling a plough. Ploughs break up and turn over hard, flat earth. They also bury weeds. This makes the ground better for planting seeds in.

Metal blades called coulters cut straight down into the ground.

These blades are called shares. They slice under the earth cut by the coulters.

At the edge of the field, the tractor lifts the plough and turns around. Then, it lowers the plough ready to start another furrow.

This board turns the sliced earth over. It is called the mouldboard.

This small ditch made by the plough is called a furrow.

Harrow

This tractor is pulling a harrow. Harrowing breaks down the big slices of earth the plough has made.

This type of harrow is called a disc harrow.

These rows of metal discs break down clods of earth as they are pulled over it.

This harrow has over 35 discs. They are arranged in rows called gangs.

Gang

The gangs are spread out behind the tractor to harrow more earth.

This metal bar is called a shaft. The harrow's discs are fixed to it.

Roller

This roller smooths the earth after harrowing. It makes the field level for planting seeds in.

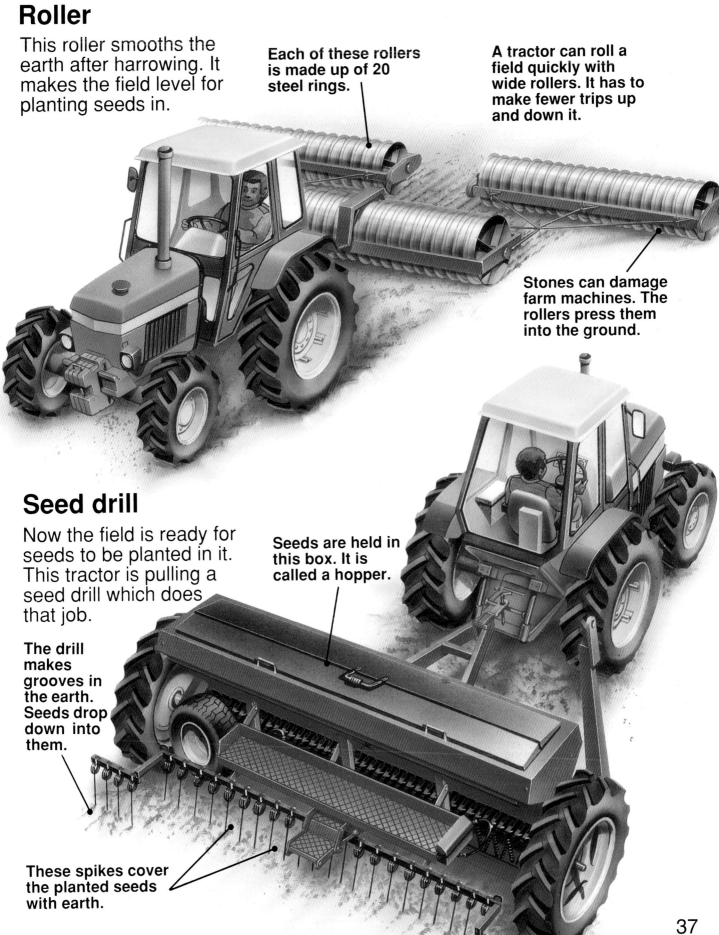

Each of these rollers is made up of 20 steel rings.

A tractor can roll a field quickly with wide rollers. It has to make fewer trips up and down it.

Stones can damage farm machines. The rollers press them into the ground.

Seed drill

Now the field is ready for seeds to be planted in it. This tractor is pulling a seed drill which does that job.

The drill makes grooves in the earth. Seeds drop down into them.

Seeds are held in this box. It is called a hopper.

These spikes cover the planted seeds with earth.

Spreaders and sprayers

Crops need food called fertilizer to grow well. They may need protection from insects and diseases, too. The machines on this page spread fertilizer over fields or spray them with pest-killing chemicals.

Muckspreader

Farm animals make a lot of muck. It is called manure or dung. It is a very good fertilizer.

A tractor pulls this machine to spread manure over crops. It is called a muckspreader.

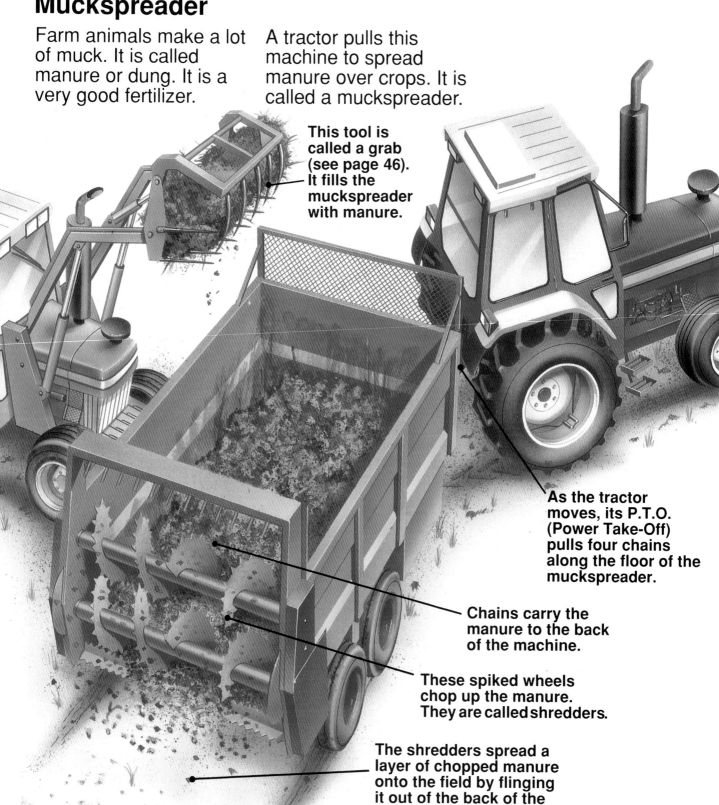

This tool is called a grab (see page 46). It fills the muckspreader with manure.

As the tractor moves, its P.T.O. (Power Take-Off) pulls four chains along the floor of the muckspreader.

Chains carry the manure to the back of the machine.

These spiked wheels chop up the manure. They are called shredders.

The shredders spread a layer of chopped manure onto the field by flinging it out of the back of the muckspreader.

Sprayer

Some farmers spray fields with chemicals called pesticides to kill insects and diseases. They are poisonous, so farmers must use them very carefully.

The machine fixed to this tractor is called a sprayer. As the tractor moves, it sprays out exactly the right amount of pesticide.

Super sprayers

In some countries, fields are huge. Farmers fix very wide sprayers behind their tractors to spray their land as quickly as possible. This sprayer is about as long as two buses.

This is an extra tank of pesticide.

Farmers do not spray pesticides on windy days. The chemicals must not blow around.

This is called the boom. It is the main part of the spraying machine.

This tank holds the pesticide mixed with some water.

The mixture is pumped through these pipes.

A pump pushes pesticide out of these tiny holes, called nozzles.

This boom has more than 20 nozzles.

Combine harvester

This farming machine is called a combine harvester. It combines two jobs in one machine. First, it cuts and gathers up crops such as wheat, peas and barley. This is called harvesting. Then it separates grains from their stalks. This is called threshing. Here you can see how it works.

Sorting out

Many crops are stalks with grains at the top. A combine cuts and pulls in the whole stalk.

Inside the cab

Some combine harvesters have computers in the cab. They tell the driver how full the grain tank is and how well the machine is working.

Information shows up on this screen.

Control panel

Metal teeth at the front of the combine push through the field. They divide it into strips.

A blade cuts the stalks off at the bottom. It makes about 1,000 cuts a minute.

This wheel, called a reel, spins around. It is covered with metal spikes called tines.

The tines push the cut stalks into the combine harvester.

Inside the machine, a stone trap catches any stones.

Drum

Box

Inside the combine, a spinning drum shakes the grains off the stalks. They collect in a box.

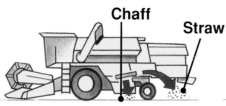

Chaff

Straw

The stalks are pushed out of the back as straw. Fans blow out waste bits called chaff.

Trailer

The grain is unloaded into a trailer. A tractor will pull it to a dry barn to be stored.

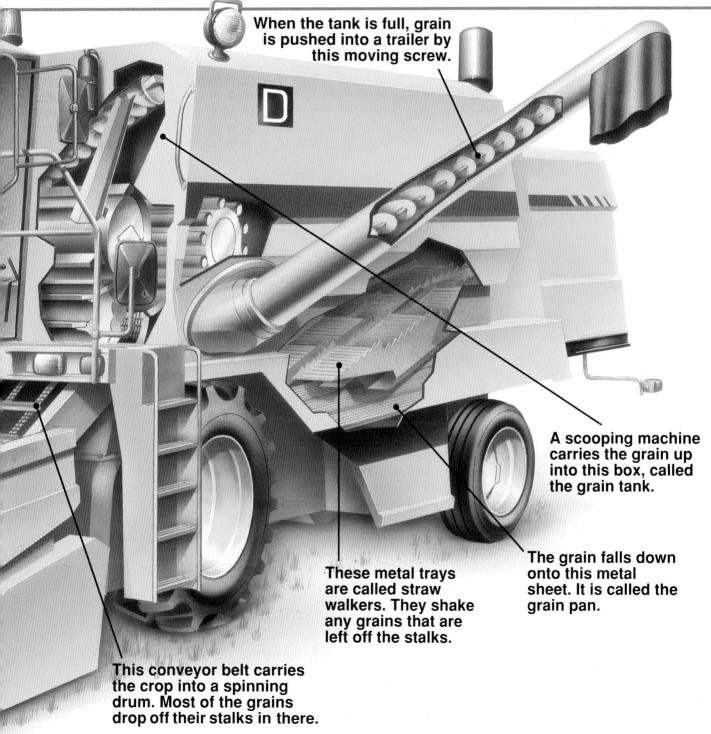

When the tank is full, grain is pushed into a trailer by this moving screw.

A scooping machine carries the grain up into this box, called the grain tank.

The grain falls down onto this metal sheet. It is called the grain pan.

These metal trays are called straw walkers. They shake any grains that are left off the stalks.

This conveyor belt carries the crop into a spinning drum. Most of the grains drop off their stalks in there.

41

Hay and straw

Farmers use these machines to cut and gather hay and straw. Straw is used as bedding for farm animals. Hay is dried grass, which they eat.

Mower

This tractor is pulling a grass mower. The mower cuts grass and leaves it in rows called swaths on the field.

These blades spin around about 3,000 times in a minute. They cut the grass.

Swath

Power from the tractor's P.T.O. goes through this metal arm to make the blades turn.

Swath turner

Straw and grass must be completely dry before they are made into bundles called bales. This tool is called a swath turner. It helps dry swaths out by turning them over.

These are swath boards. They can move in or out to make thinner or fatter swaths.

These wheels are called finger wheels. They pick up grass in the swath and turn it over.

Baler

Wrapping hay and straw into bales makes it easier to carry them around. This machine makes round bales. It is called a round baler.

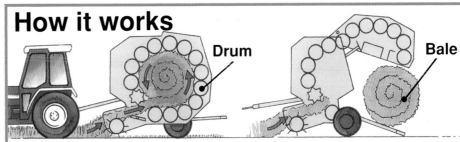

How it works

Drum

Bale

Metal fingers at the front of the baler push hay and straw into the machine. Spinning drums roll them into a ball.

String ties the bale up tight. Then the top half of the baler opens. The new bale falls out of the back onto the field.

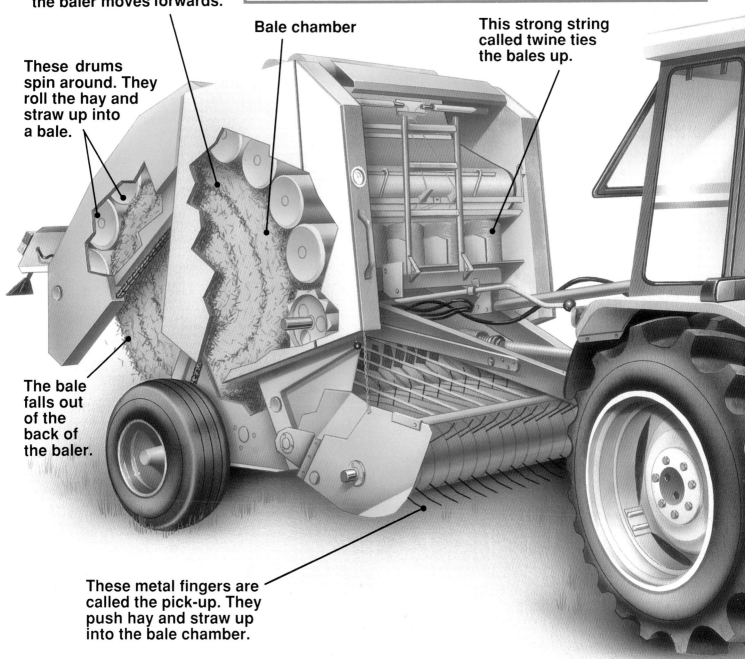

Straw and hay are pushed up into here as the baler moves forwards.

Bale chamber

This strong string called twine ties the bales up.

These drums spin around. They roll the hay and straw up into a bale.

The bale falls out of the back of the baler.

These metal fingers are called the pick-up. They push hay and straw up into the bale chamber.

Feeding animals

In the summer, animals can eat grass or crops grown for them. This sort of animal food is called forage. Farmers harvest forage crops in the summer and make them into a food called silage. They can feed this to their animals in winter, when less forage grows.

Forage to silage

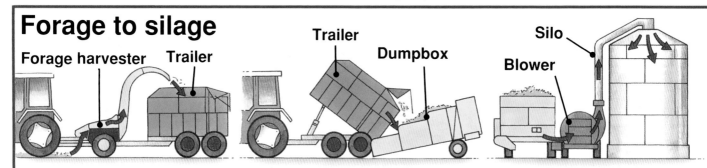

Forage harvester   **Trailer**   **Trailer**   **Dumpbox**   **Silo**   **Blower**

The forage harvester picks up cut grass. It chops it up and blows it into a trailer.

The chopped-up forage is tipped into a metal box called a dumpbox back in the farmyard.

A blower blows forage into a tower called a silo. Inside here, it slowly becomes silage.

Forage harvester

This machine is a forage harvester. It picks up forage crops and chops them up as it moves.

This is the pick-up. It spins around very fast, picking up forage with metal spikes called tines.

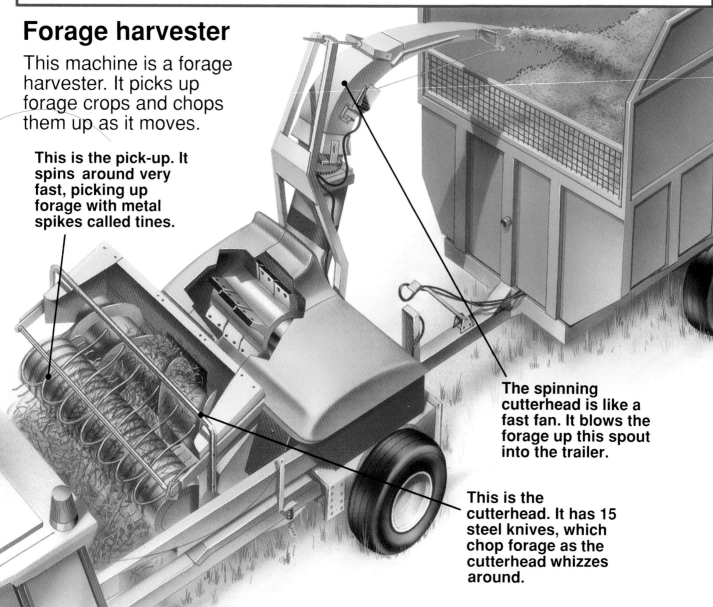

The spinning cutterhead is like a fast fan. It blows the forage up this spout into the trailer.

This is the cutterhead. It has 15 steel knives, which chop forage as the cutterhead whizzes around.

Dumpbox and blower

At one end of the dumpbox, a blower blows forage into the tower silo with a powerful fan. Inside the silo, forage pickles as if it was in vinegar. This turns it into silage.

A silo must be completely sealed. No air must get in. This makes forage pickle better.

The silo is sealed shut all summer while the forage becomes silage.

A moving metal belt carries the forage up to the other end of the dumpbox.

It is dangerous to go into a silo. Silage gives off smelly gases so there is no air inside for humans to breathe.

These toothed wheels turn around. They push the forage towards the blower.

This is the blower. It needs power from a tractor's P.T.O. to make it work.

The forage is blown very fast up this pipe.

It takes about 45 minutes to blow all the silage out of the dumpbox into the silo.

Lifters

Farmers fix tools to the front of tractors as well as to the back of them. These tools are specially built to lift and carry around the farm.

Grab

This tool is called a grab. The farmer can fix it to his tractor to pick up and move silage or manure.

This is the grab.

These prongs are called tines. They are arranged like rows of teeth.

The tractor driver controls the grab with levers inside the cab.

These extra tines stop anything from falling out of the side of the grab.

How the grab works

Tines

When the grab is near the manure, the driver pulls a lever. Its tines open up like a mouth.

Another lever makes the tines close around some manure. The grab lifts up with its load.

The tines open to let the manure fall out where the driver wants to unload it.

Bale fork

Bales of hay and straw are heavy and difficult to lift. Farmers fix a tool called a bale fork to their tractor to move them around the farm.

This spike sticks deep into the bale.

This metal pedal pushes the bale off the spikes.

This smaller spike stops the bale swaying from side to side as the tractor drives along.

Fork-lift tractor

Farmers need to move sacks of grain, cattle food or fertilizer around the farm. They can fix a fork-lift to the front of a tractor to do this.

How it works

As the tractor moves forwards, the fork sticks into the bale.

Bale

Fork

The bale fork lifts up to carry loads, so that the farmer can see the road.

The tractor lowers the bale fork. A pedal pushes the bale off.

Pedal

Boom

These two prongs are called forks. They are on the end of a metal arm called a boom. Together, they make the fork-lift.

Sacks rest on wooden trays laid on top of the forks.

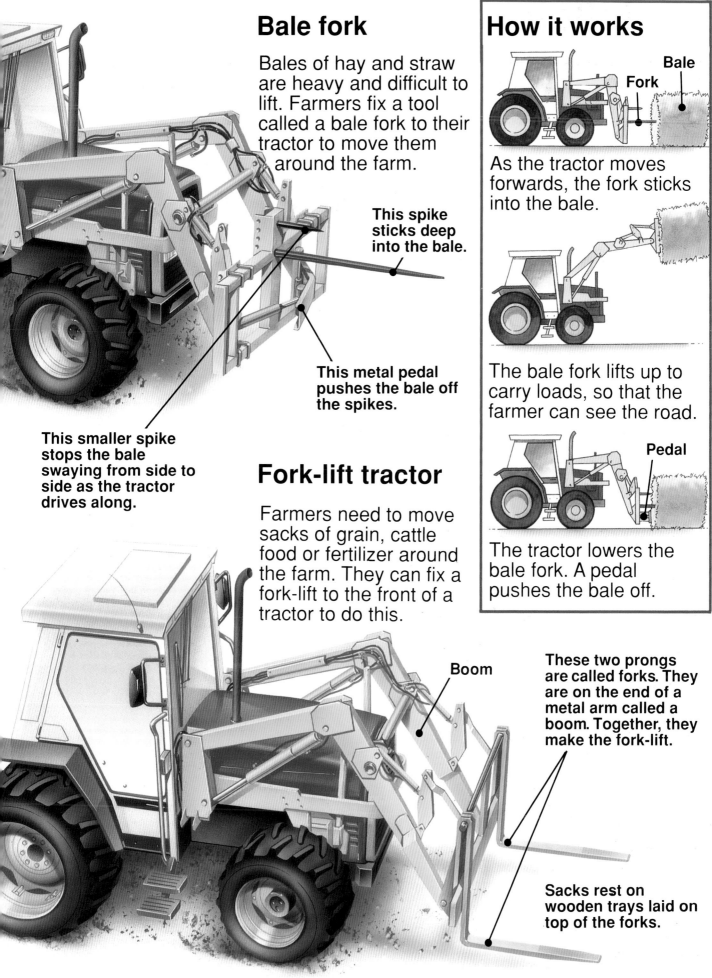

47

Root crop machines

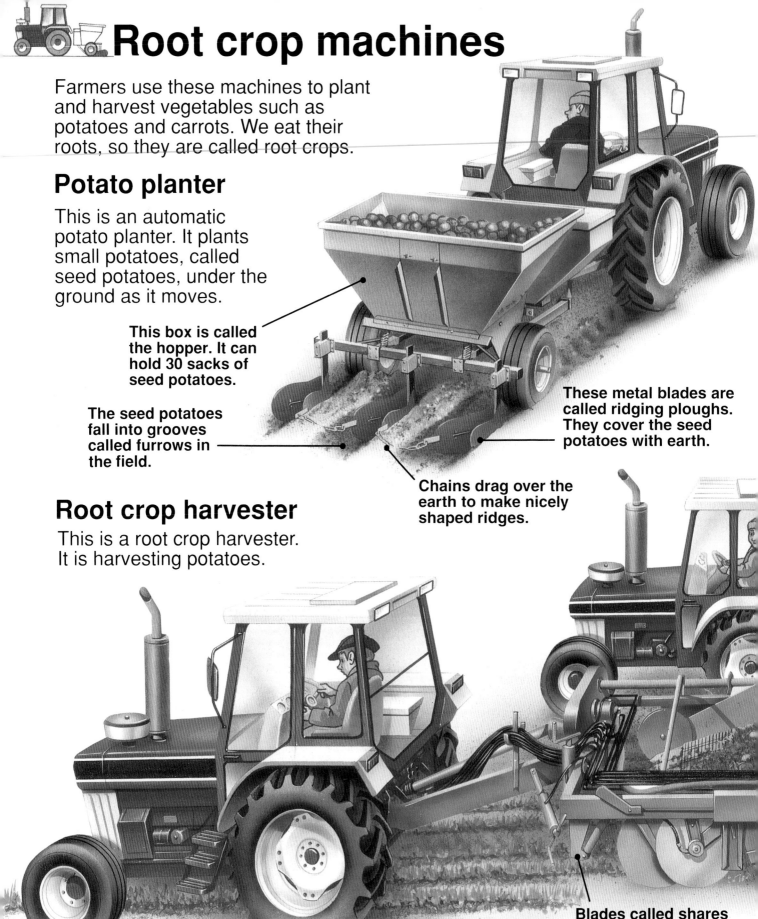

Farmers use these machines to plant and harvest vegetables such as potatoes and carrots. We eat their roots, so they are called root crops.

Potato planter

This is an automatic potato planter. It plants small potatoes, called seed potatoes, under the ground as it moves.

This box is called the hopper. It can hold 30 sacks of seed potatoes.

The seed potatoes fall into grooves called furrows in the field.

These metal blades are called ridging ploughs. They cover the seed potatoes with earth.

Chains drag over the earth to make nicely shaped ridges.

Root crop harvester

This is a root crop harvester. It is harvesting potatoes.

The tractor guides the harvester between the rows of potato plants.

Blades called shares slice under the potatoes. They lift the whole plant out of the ground.

Inside the machine

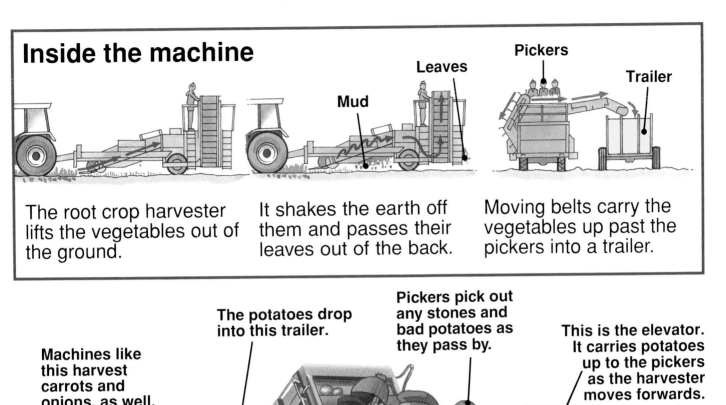

The root crop harvester lifts the vegetables out of the ground.

It shakes the earth off them and passes their leaves out of the back.

Moving belts carry the vegetables up past the pickers into a trailer.

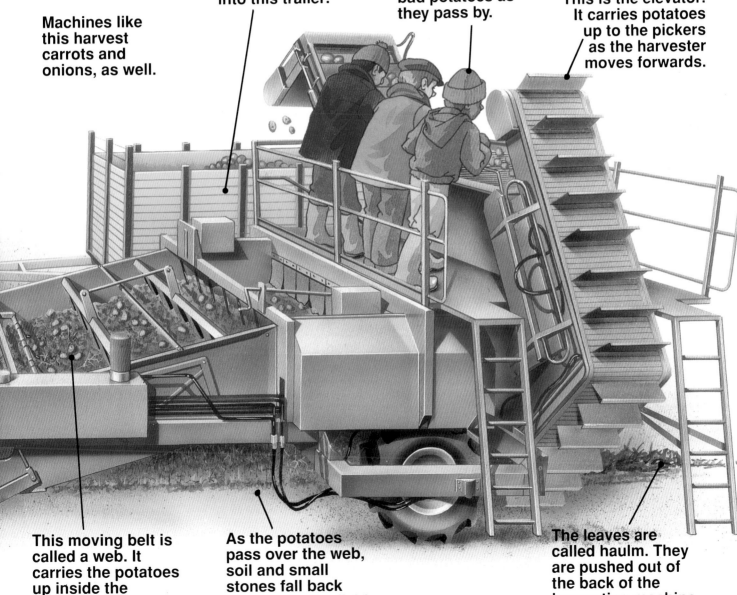

Machines like this harvest carrots and onions, as well.

The potatoes drop into this trailer.

Pickers pick out any stones and bad potatoes as they pass by.

This is the elevator. It carries potatoes up to the pickers as the harvester moves forwards.

This moving belt is called a web. It carries the potatoes up inside the harvester.

As the potatoes pass over the web, soil and small stones fall back down onto the field.

The leaves are called haulm. They are pushed out of the back of the harvesting machine.

Giant tractor

Ordinary tractors are not powerful enough for some farming jobs. Huge machines like this do them. This tractor usually works in the big wheat fields of North America. It can work for a long time without stopping.

Wheels and weight

Tractors like this are very heavy. They need eight wheels to carry their enormous weight.

All eight tyres turn together to make the huge tractor move and turn around.

The tractor's tyres are very wide. This helps them grip more ground to pull the tractor along.

Giant tractors like this are heavy and slow. They can only go about as fast as a bicycle.

This tractor can pull heavy loads and other farming tools behind it, too.

Headlights

Big Bud

This is one of the biggest tractors in the world. It is called Big Bud. Its tyres are taller than a man.

Big Bud was specially built to work on big farms in North America.

The eight wide tyres spread the tractor's weight out over more ground. They help stop it sinking into the field.

This tractor can work for about 24 hours without needing more fuel.

This is the air filter. It stops dust getting into the engine and damaging it.

Sitting in this cab is like looking out of an upstairs window of a house.

The driver can listen to the radio or cassettes while he works long hours.

This thick glass stops too much engine noise getting into the cab.

Giant tractors often work at night, too. They have lights at the front and at the back.

Some of the wheat fields in North America are so long that it can take an hour to drive from one end to the other.

This tractor's engine is much more powerful than an ordinary tractor's engine.

51

 # Loaders

These machines are built to pick up loads. They are called loaders. Three different types of loaders work on farms.

Tractor loader

This is a tractor loader. It has a bucket for scooping things into fixed in front of its cab.

Farmers can pick up mud, stones, manure or grain in the loader bucket.

The driver controls the loader bucket by moving a lever in the cab.

This arm is called the boom. It bends in the middle to help the bucket scoop things up.

The boom can stretch up as high as an upstairs window.

A weight on the back of the tractor stops it falling forwards when it carries heavy loads. It is called the counterweight.

The farmer can take the loader bucket off the tractor in only a few minutes.

Farmers can fix other tools to the front of loaders. You can see some on pages 46 and 47.

Skid-steer loader

This skid-steer loader does smaller loading jobs. It is called a skid-steer loader because it can turn around so quickly and easily it is like skidding.

Skid-steer loaders can stop and spin around to face the other way in a very small space.

The driver sits in this small cab.

Metal bars called rollbars protect him in case the loader topples over.

The driver controls the loader with foot pedals in the cab.

Telescopic loader

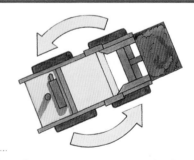

Lifting arm

Loaders like this are called telescopic loaders. On these machines, the lifting arm slides out from inside a straight metal case, just like a telescope does.

Lift and load

Boom

Bucket

A skid-steer loader can scoop things up when its bucket tilts like this.

Its boom can reach up and unload things high above the cab.

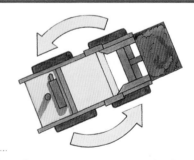

The farmer can steer the loader so that it turns around in a circle.

Around the farm

Tractors do many unusual jobs on a farm. Here, they have tools fixed to them for digging ditches, cutting hedges and banging in fence posts.

Ditch digger

If a field stays too wet after rain, crops cannot grow in it. The farmer must get the water off the field, or drain it.

This tractor is using a tool called a backhoe to dig drainage ditches. The water will flow off the field and into the ditches.

Hedge-trimmer

Farmers have to keep hedges tidy. This tractor has an arm called a hedge-trimmer fixed to it. As the tractor moves, the trimmer's metal blades cut the tops off hedges.

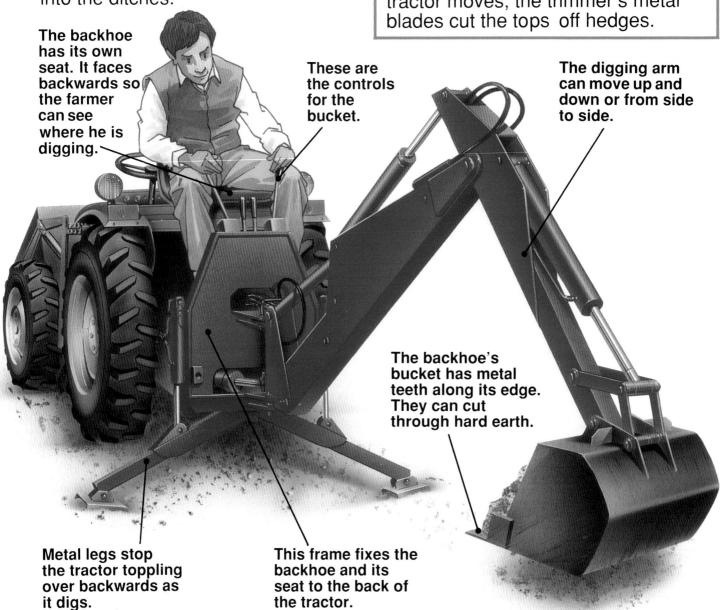

The backhoe has its own seat. It faces backwards so the farmer can see where he is digging.

These are the controls for the bucket.

The digging arm can move up and down or from side to side.

The backhoe's bucket has metal teeth along its edge. They can cut through hard earth.

Metal legs stop the tractor toppling over backwards as it digs.

This frame fixes the backhoe and its seat to the back of the tractor.

Post driver

Tractors can help the farmer put fences around his fields. This tractor has a tool called a post driver fixed to it. It pushes fence posts into the ground. The farmer joins them up with wire.

This metal frame fixes the post driver to the back of the tractor. It is very strong.

This heavy weight is like a hammer. It bangs the posts into the ground.

Post drivers are sometimes called post bashers.

Pushing power

Post

The farmer slides a wooden post into a slot in the post driver.

He puts the post driver above the place where he wants a fence post.

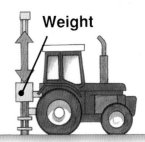
Weight

Heavy weights slide down the driver and bang the post into the ground.

Some frames can swing around to work on either side of the tractor.

This post driver can bash in a post every 40 seconds.

Post

These metal legs are called stabilizers. They hold the tractor steady as it thumps in posts.

55

Crawler tractor

This tractor has rubber tracks instead of tyres. They are called crawler tracks. Farmers use crawler tractors like this in wet, muddy fields where ordinary tractors might get stuck. They can also pull heavy loads and farming tools without their tracks slipping or sinking.

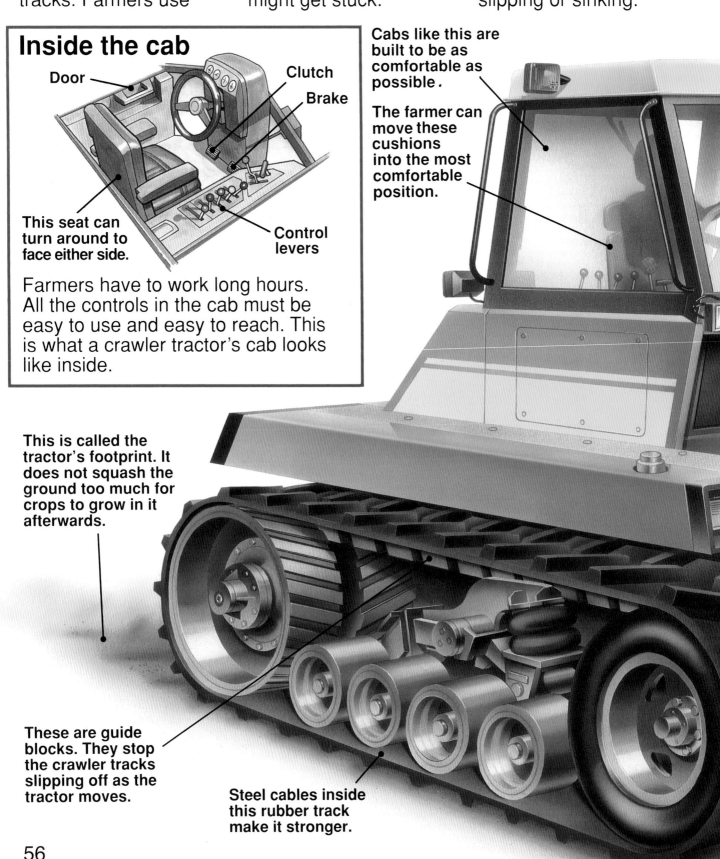

Inside the cab

Door

Clutch

Brake

This seat can turn around to face either side.

Control levers

Farmers have to work long hours. All the controls in the cab must be easy to use and easy to reach. This is what a crawler tractor's cab looks like inside.

Cabs like this are built to be as comfortable as possible.

The farmer can move these cushions into the most comfortable position.

This is called the tractor's footprint. It does not squash the ground too much for crops to grow in it afterwards.

These are guide blocks. They stop the crawler tracks slipping off as the tractor moves.

Steel cables inside this rubber track make it stronger.

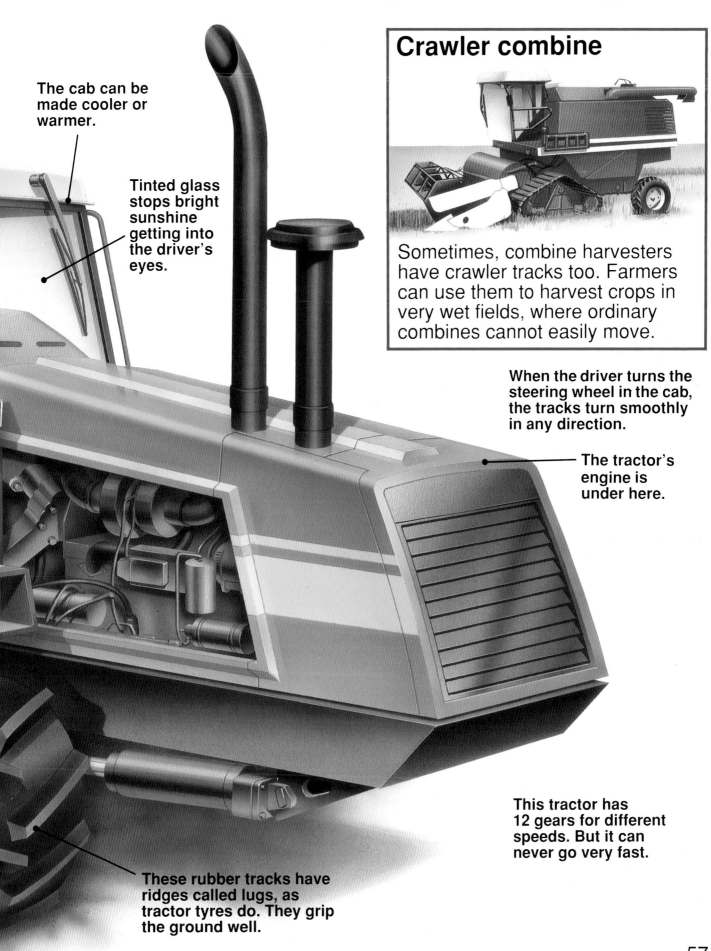

The cab can be made cooler or warmer.

Tinted glass stops bright sunshine getting into the driver's eyes.

Crawler combine

Sometimes, combine harvesters have crawler tracks too. Farmers can use them to harvest crops in very wet fields, where ordinary combines cannot easily move.

When the driver turns the steering wheel in the cab, the tracks turn smoothly in any direction.

The tractor's engine is under here.

This tractor has 12 gears for different speeds. But it can never go very fast.

These rubber tracks have ridges called lugs, as tractor tyres do. They grip the ground well.

Fruit-farming machines

Farmers who grow fruit need different sorts of farming machines. You can see two of them here.

Currant harvester

Fruit can easily be damaged when it is picked. Then it is not worth as much money.

This machine harvests blackcurrants and redcurrants without squashing them.

Looking inside

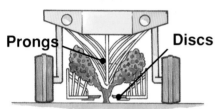

Prongs　　**Discs**

The branches of each bush are pushed into two halves by metal prongs and plastic discs.

Tray

Fingers

Plastic fingers above the discs gently tap each bush. Berries drop off into trays.

Picker

The trays slowly move, carrying the berries up to pickers. They pack the fruit into boxes.

The driver drives the machine very slowly over the bushes.

These plastic fingers knock the berries off.

The bushes push these bendy discs back as they go into the machine.

These metal prongs part the bush into two, like hair.

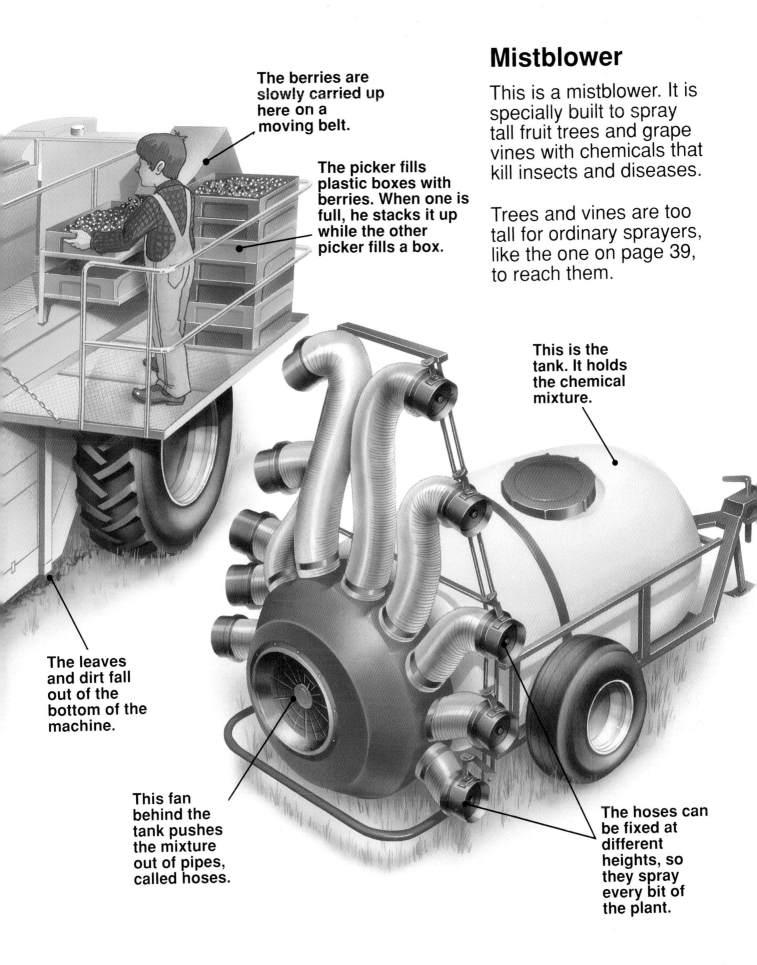

The berries are slowly carried up here on a moving belt.

The picker fills plastic boxes with berries. When one is full, he stacks it up while the other picker fills a box.

The leaves and dirt fall out of the bottom of the machine.

This fan behind the tank pushes the mixture out of pipes, called hoses.

Mistblower

This is a mistblower. It is specially built to spray tall fruit trees and grape vines with chemicals that kill insects and diseases.

Trees and vines are too tall for ordinary sprayers, like the one on page 39, to reach them.

This is the tank. It holds the chemical mixture.

The hoses can be fixed at different heights, so they spray every bit of the plant.

Special tractors

Farmers need different tractors for different jobs. The ones on this page are built to do special sorts of work.

Three-wheeler

This tractor has three huge wheels. They hold so much air that the tractor does not squash the soil.

Its job is to spread fertilizer over big fields just before seeds are planted in them.

This light flashes when the tractor is moving on roads.

This tractor's cab is much higher above the ground than on ordinary tractors.

This trailer is full of fertilizer.

These big, round tyres spread the tractor's weight over the field.

The engine is under the cab, not in front of it. This means that all three wheels help spread out its weight.

Mini-tractor

This tractor is too small for farm-work. People use mini-tractors like this to mow the grass on golf-courses, in parks or in large gardens.

Narrow tractor

Tractors like this can work between rows of grapevines or fruit trees. They are very narrow, so that they don't damage any crops.

These tractors are about half as wide as ordinary tractors.

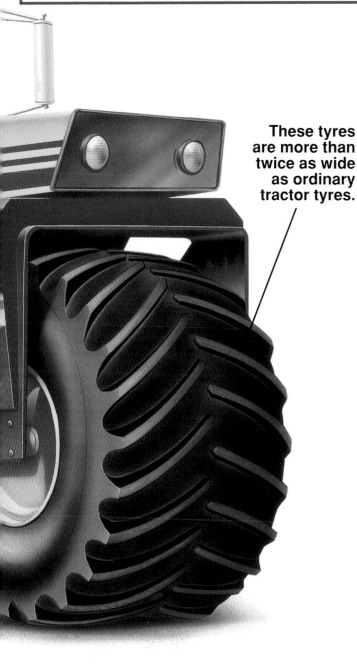

These tyres are more than twice as wide as ordinary tractor tyres.

A.T.V.

This A.T.V. can go as fast as an ordinary motorbike.

Some farmers ride around their fields on bikes like these. They are called A.T.V.s. This is short for All-Terrain Vehicle, which means they can go over any sort of ground.

Tractors old and new

Farming has changed a lot in the last 100 years. Tractors and other farming machines make the farmer's job much easier than it used to be.

On these two pages you can see some of the first tractors, as well as some of the newest farm machines that work in the fields today.

Early tractor

This tractor was built in Canada around 80 years ago. At that time, more and more farmers started using machines to do their farm-work.

This tractor uses a fuel called kerosene to make it work.

These wheels are made of solid metal. They have ridges cut into them to help them to grip, though.

This type of tractor can use petrol in its engine.

Three wheeler

This tractor was built in 1914. It only has three wheels. It was popular because it was tough and cheap to run.

This tractor is called 'The Bull'.

Lighter tractor

By the 1930s, many tractors looked like this. They have rubber tyres. These are lighter than metal ones are which makes tractors easier to drive.

Rubber tyres grip the ground better than metal wheels.

Systems tractor

This machine works on many farms in Europe today. It is called a systems tractor. Farmers fix tools to the front, middle and back of it, so it can do three jobs at once.

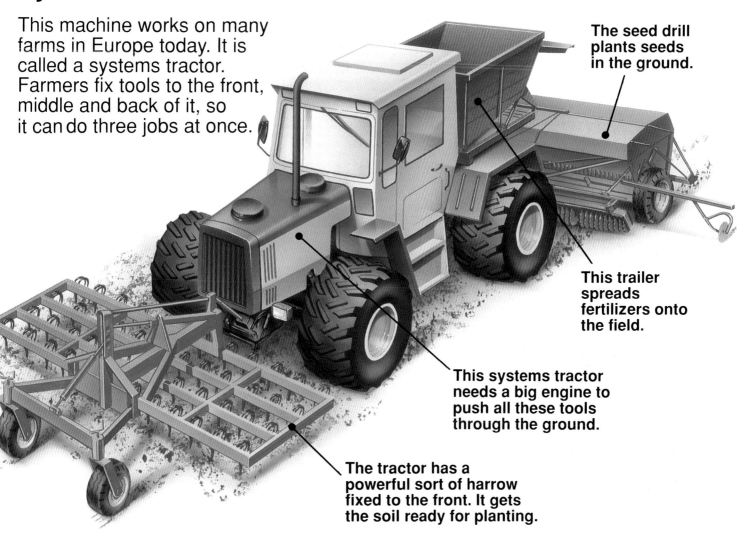

The seed drill plants seeds in the ground.

This trailer spreads fertilizers onto the field.

This systems tractor needs a big engine to push all these tools through the ground.

The tractor has a powerful sort of harrow fixed to the front. It gets the soil ready for planting.

Gantry

This wide machine is called a gantry. It farms big fields without squashing the soil by making too many trips up and down it.

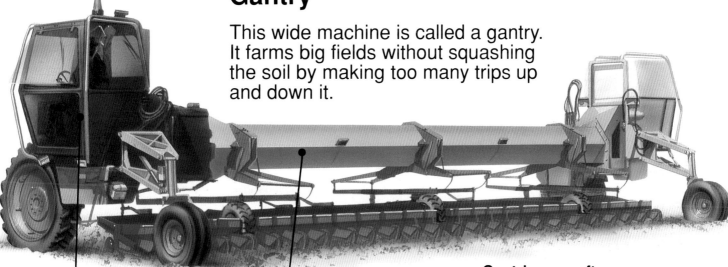

The driver sits in this cab. He has a clear view of the field and the gantry as he drives.

Some gantries are as long as six men lying down head to toe.

Gantries are often used by farmers who grow flowers. This sort of farming is called horticulture.

Picture Puzzle

These are parts of some of the tractors and their tools that are in this part of the book. Can you remember what they are called? The answers are at the bottom of the page.

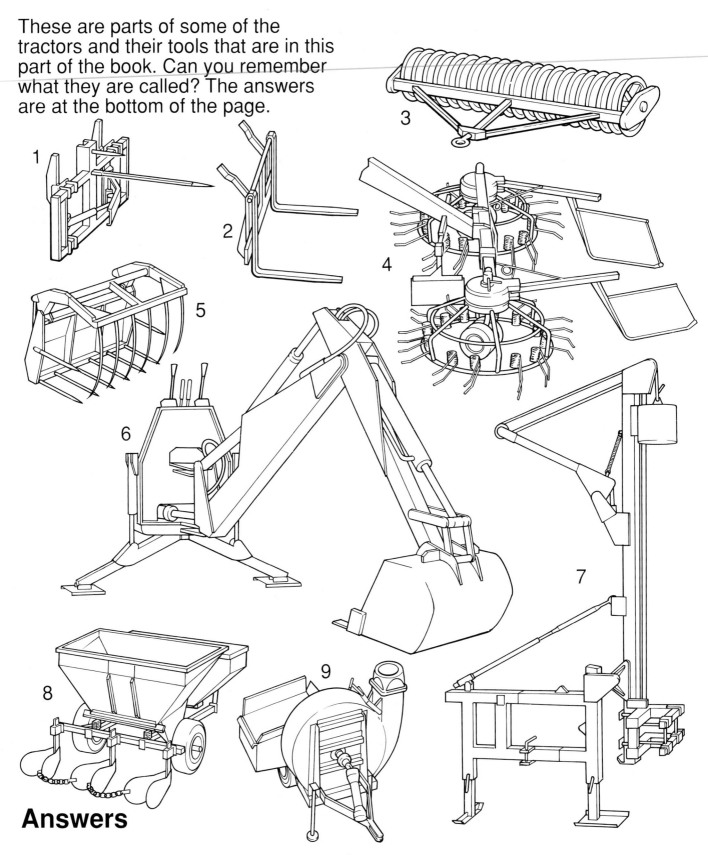

Answers

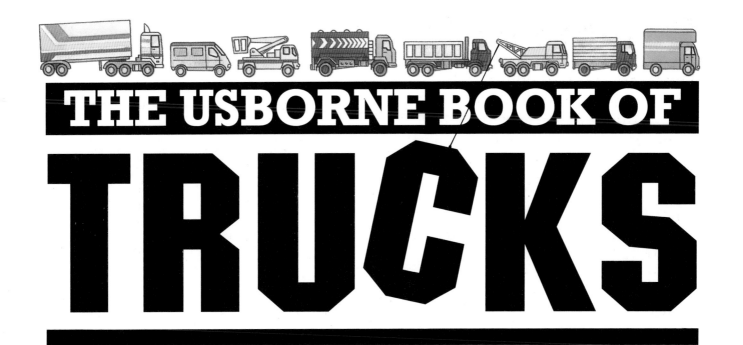

THE USBORNE BOOK OF
TRUCKS

Harriet Castor

Designed by Robert Walster

Illustrated by Chris Lyon, Sean Wilkinson and Teri Gower

Consultant: Gibb Grace
(Product and Environmental Affairs Manager, Leyland DAF Ltd)

Contents

 # Truck

Trucks are used for taking all sorts of things from one place to another. They often carry very heavy loads, so they need to have powerful engines and strong bodies.

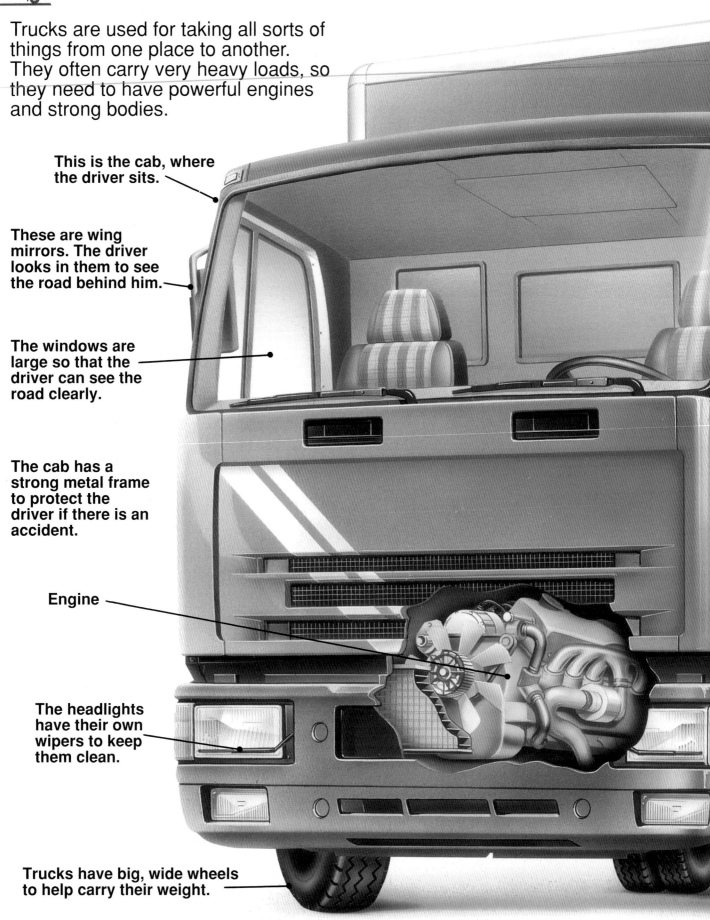

This is the cab, where the driver sits.

These are wing mirrors. The driver looks in them to see the road behind him.

The windows are large so that the driver can see the road clearly.

The cab has a strong metal frame to protect the driver if there is an accident.

Engine

The headlights have their own wipers to keep them clean.

Trucks have big, wide wheels to help carry their weight.

This is the body of the truck. The load is put in here.

The main frame of the truck is called the chassis. It is made of strong steel.

There are double wheels at the back for extra support.

Different bodies

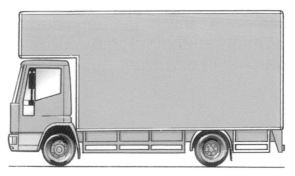

This truck's body is like a big box. It has extra space above the cab.

This truck's flat body is called a flatbed. The load goes on top.

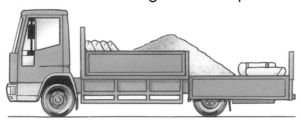

This truck has low sides which fold down to make unloading easier.

Engine check

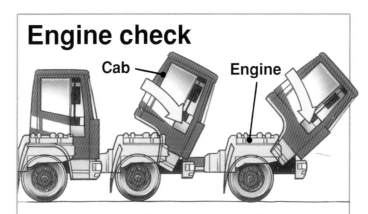

Cab   Engine

When the engine needs to be checked, the cab can be tilted forward. This makes the engine easy to reach.

Articulated and rigid trucks

There are two main types of truck: articulated trucks, or artics, and rigid trucks. Artics have two separate parts, which can be joined together and taken apart again. Rigid trucks are all in one piece.

On the body it often says who the truck belongs to and what is inside.

Artic

The two parts of the artic are linked. The link lets the cab turn first when it goes around corners.

The back part of the artic is called the semi-trailer.

The semi-trailer can stand by itself when these metal legs are put down.

The semi-trailer locks onto a big metal plate here.

The front part of the artic is called the tractor unit.

Swapping semi-trailers

Tractor unit drives away.

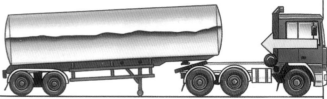

Tractor unit backs up to the new semi-trailer.

When the artic arrives, its tractor unit and semi-trailer are taken apart. The driver does not unload the semi-trailer. He leaves it behind.

A new semi-trailer is put on. Now the artic is ready for its next journey. This saves time, so the artic can make more deliveries.

Curtainsider

Here is one type of rigid truck. It has a special body, with sides that pull back like curtains. It is called a curtainsider.

This shaped panel helps the truck push through the air when it is going fast.

The sides of this truck fasten here with buckles.

The curtainsider is loaded by a forklift truck.

The curtains can be drawn back all the way along the sides.

Most trucks only open at the back. Curtainsiders are easier to load.

 # Tanker

A tanker has a body like a big can. Tankers can carry liquids, powders and gases. They often carry fuels such as petrol and diesel. This tanker is delivering to a petrol station.

The compartments stop the liquid from sloshing around too much.

This compartment has petrol in it.

Inside the tanker there are separate boxes called compartments.

This compartment has diesel in it.

These curved sides are stronger than the flat sides on normal trucks.

This is a warning sign. Find out what it means below.

Petrol and diesel catch fire easily. Tanker-drivers are trained to deal with emergencies.

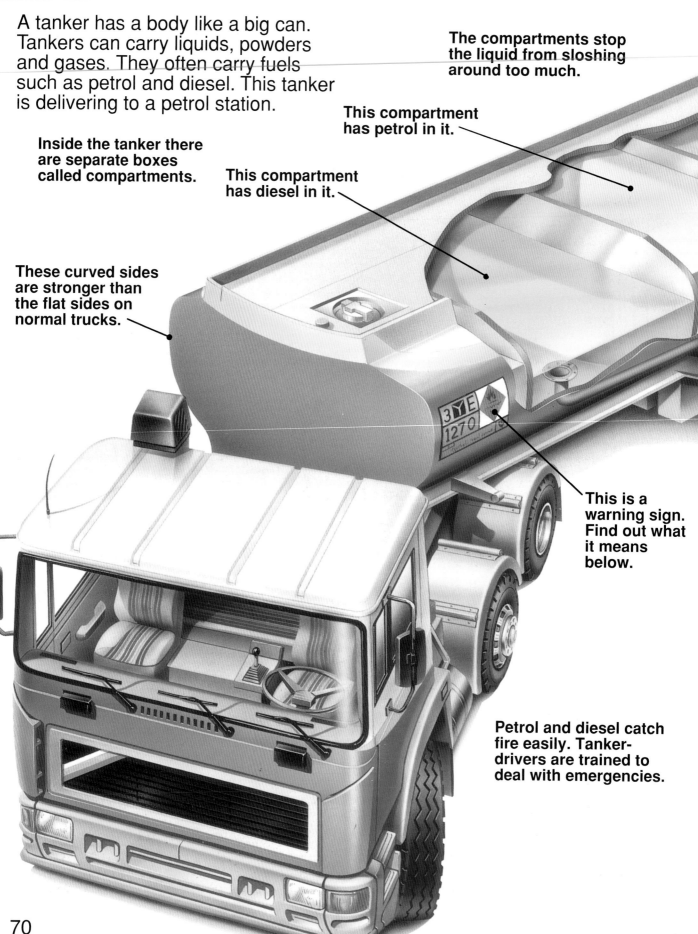

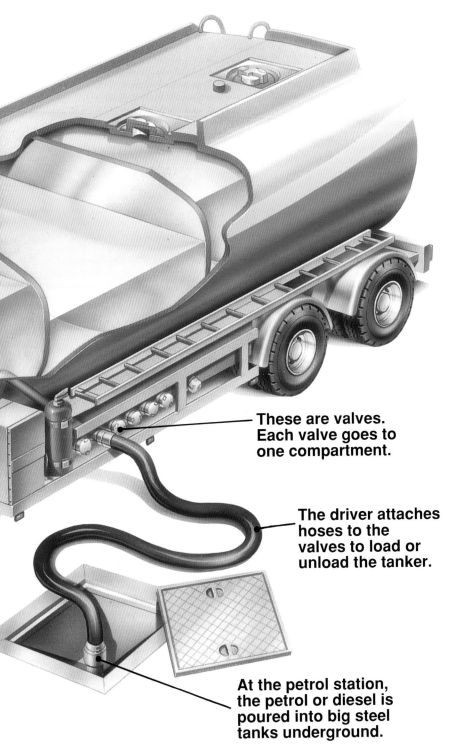

These are valves. Each valve goes to one compartment.

The driver attaches hoses to the valves to load or unload the tanker.

At the petrol station, the petrol or diesel is poured into big steel tanks underground.

Tanker delivery

Hose

Storage tank

A hose from the tanker is put down into the storage tank. The petrol pours in.

Petrol pump

Petrol goes this way.

When someone uses the petrol pump, the petrol goes along a pipe and into the car's fuel tank.

Warning signs

Tankers have signs on them to show what is inside. Then if the tanker catches fire, the firefighters will know right away how to put out the flames.

FLAMMABLE LIQUID

A flammable liquid is one that can catch fire. This sign is used on fuel tankers.

FLAMMABLE SOLID

This sign shows that the load is something solid that can catch fire.

TOXIC GAS

This sign shows that the tanker is carrying a toxic, or poisonous, gas.

Dump truck

Dump trucks have bodies that tilt so that the load slides out. This giant dump truck is working at a quarry.

This board protects the cab from falling rocks.

Dumping

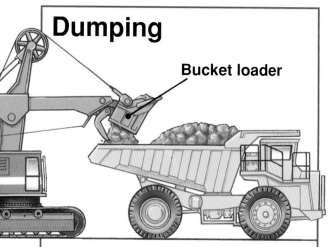

Bucket loader

The dump truck is loaded by a big bucket loader. It fills the back with rocks.

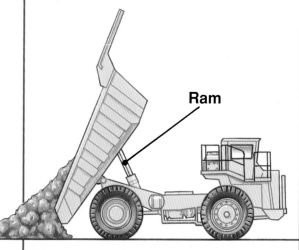

Ram

To empty the dump truck an arm called a ram lifts up the body. The load slides out.

The driver climbs this ladder to reach the cab.

Different dump trucks

Not all dump trucks are the same. Dump trucks of different sizes are used for carrying different loads, such as gravel, sand or fruit. Sometimes smaller dump trucks are called tippers. You can see three of them here.

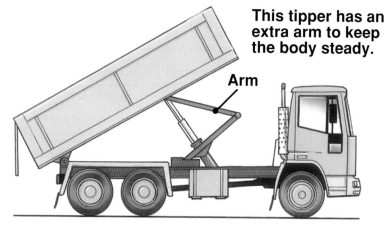

This tipper has an extra arm to keep the body steady.

Arm

72

This dump truck is too big to travel on normal roads.

The rocks are loaded in here.

This is the tallest truck in this book. Its wheels are twice as high as a tall person.

This slope stops the load from falling out when the truck is not dumping.

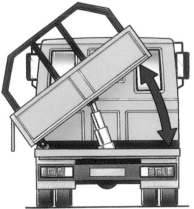

This tipper can dump its load sideways.

This tipper's extra long ram lifts the body up very high.

Wrecker

This truck is used when a car breaks down or has an accident. The truck can lift the car back onto the road. Then it can tow the car away.

This arm is called a boom.

The driver works the winch with these switches.

This cable is made of metal wire. It is very strong.

These metal rods are lifting rams. They hold the boom up.

These lights are used if the truck is working at night.

These metal legs dig into the ground to help keep the truck still.

Muscle power

The first wreckers just carried equipment. This one was used in 1914. The crew did the lifting themselves, with ropes, chains and a metal tripod.

Tripod   Wrecker

This drum is called a winch. It winds in the cable, pulling the car up.

Tools are kept in here.

This truck can lift loads as heavy as 12 big elephants.

Towing

The wrecker can tow things as big as itself, like this bus.

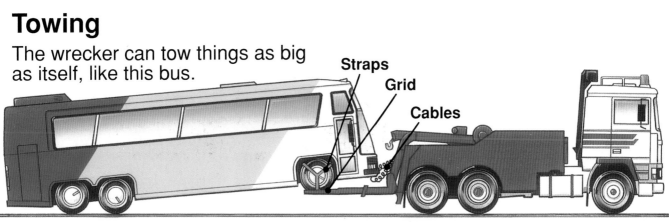

Straps

Grid

Cables

The bus's front wheels are lifted onto a metal frame called a grid. They are tied on with straps.

Cables carry power from the truck's engine to the bus. This makes the bus's brakes and lights work.

Car transporter

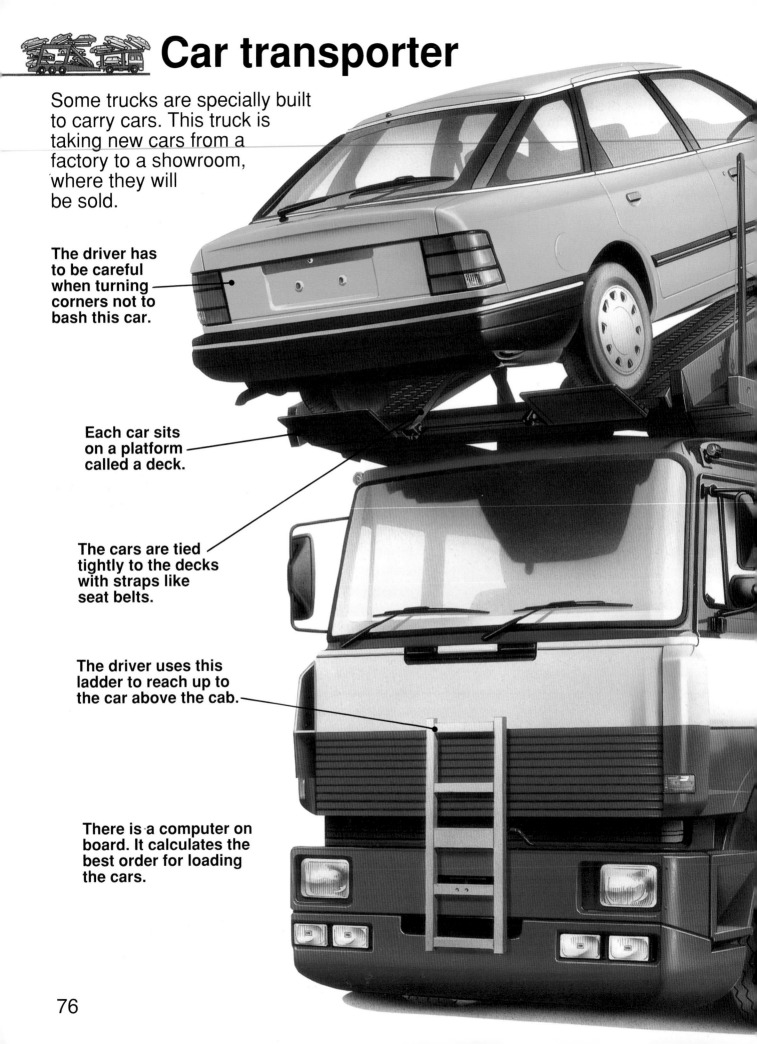

Some trucks are specially built to carry cars. This truck is taking new cars from a factory to a showroom, where they will be sold.

The driver has to be careful when turning corners not to bash this car.

Each car sits on a platform called a deck.

The cars are tied tightly to the decks with straps like seat belts.

The driver uses this ladder to reach up to the car above the cab.

There is a computer on board. It calculates the best order for loading the cars.

This transporter can carry 12 large cars.

Early transporter

This transporter was built in 1948. It can only carry four cars at a time.

The decks are tilted so that more cars can fit onto the transporter.

The cars are driven onto the transporter from the back.

The semi-trailer is very low to the ground so that more layers of cars can fit on.

It takes about an hour to load the transporter.

# Racing car transporter

This truck carries racing cars inside its big semi-trailer. When it gets to a race, the truck is used as a workshop. It carries all the tools and spare parts that might be needed to repair the cars.

Races are held all over the world, so the transporter travels vast distances every year.

The outside of the truck is painted with the name and colours of the racing team.

The cars have different types of tyres for dry and wet weather.

Spare wheels are kept inside these big lockers.

Inside the truck there is room for three cars. They are carried on two levels (see the opposite page).

The cars are lifted into and out of the truck on this platform.

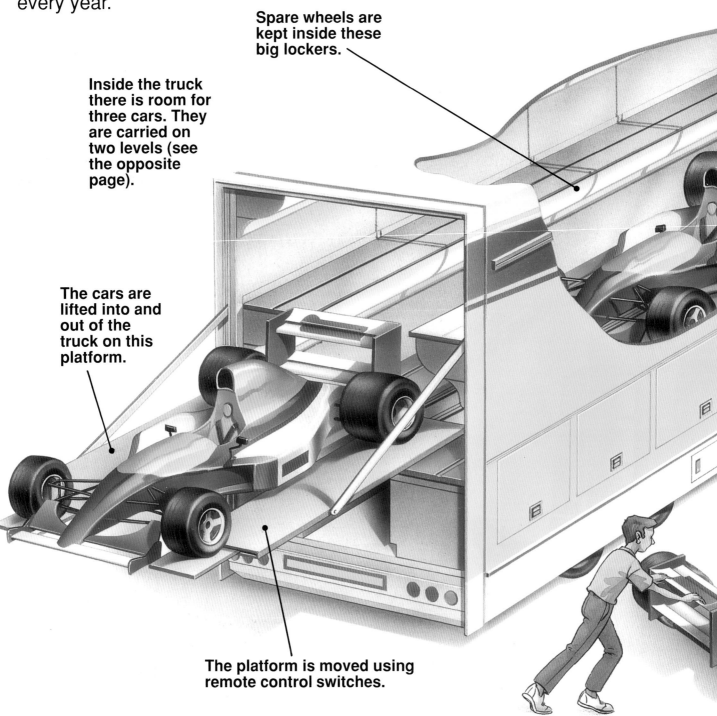

The platform is moved using remote control switches.

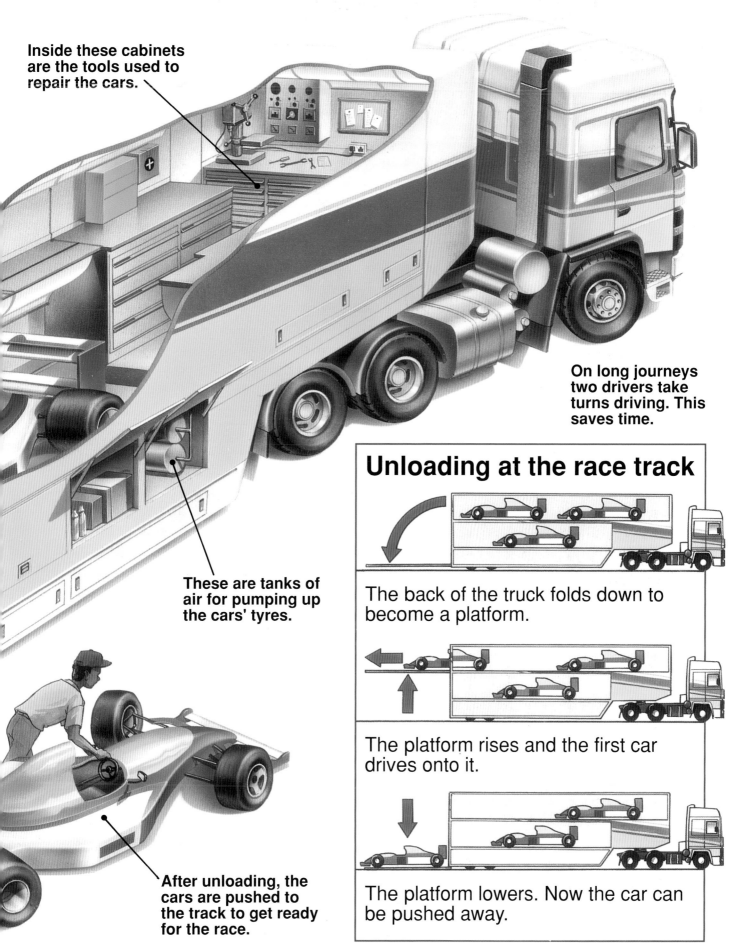

Inside these cabinets are the tools used to repair the cars.

On long journeys two drivers take turns driving. This saves time.

These are tanks of air for pumping up the cars' tyres.

After unloading, the cars are pushed to the track to get ready for the race.

Unloading at the race track

The back of the truck folds down to become a platform.

The platform rises and the first car drives onto it.

The platform lowers. Now the car can be pushed away.

79

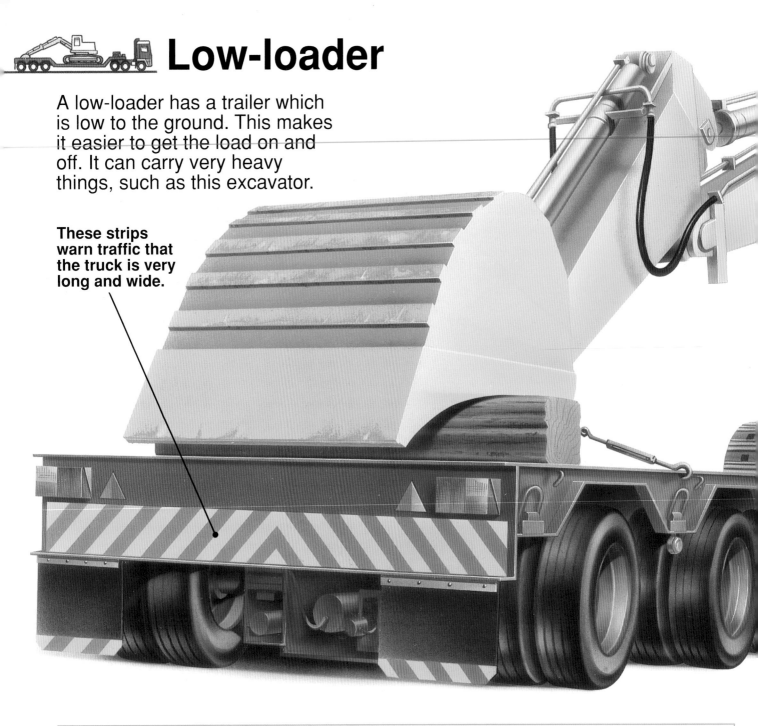

Low-loader

A low-loader has a trailer which is low to the ground. This makes it easier to get the load on and off. It can carry very heavy things, such as this excavator.

These strips warn traffic that the truck is very long and wide.

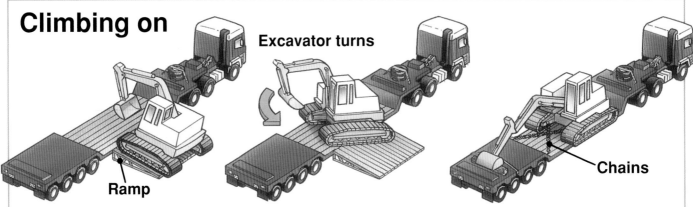

Climbing on

Excavator turns

Ramp

Chains

The excavator climbs up a ramp onto the trailer.

Then it turns on the spot to face the other way.

It is tied to the trailer with chains.

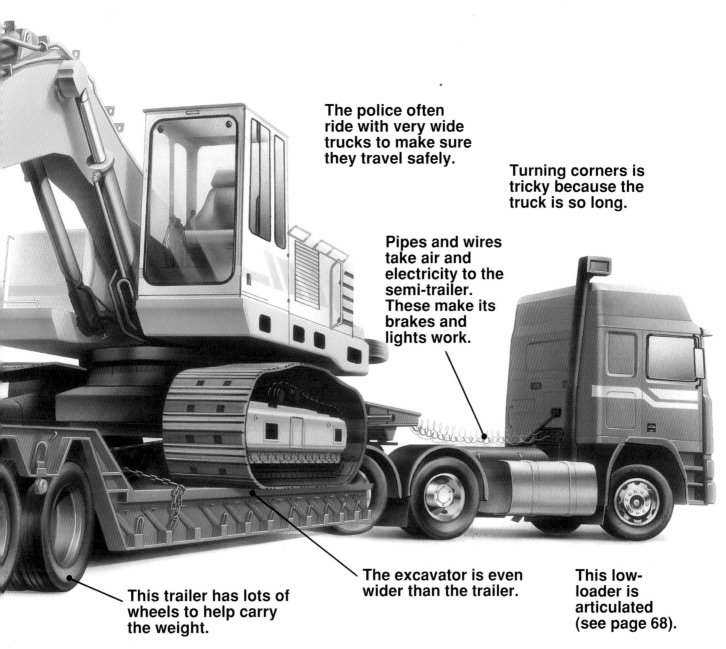

The police often ride with very wide trucks to make sure they travel safely.

Turning corners is tricky because the truck is so long.

Pipes and wires take air and electricity to the semi-trailer. These make its brakes and lights work.

The excavator is even wider than the trailer.

This low-loader is articulated (see page 68).

This trailer has lots of wheels to help carry the weight.

Space Shuttle truck

One of the largest loads carried by a truck is this Space Shuttle orbiter. The truck drives it to the launching pad.

The truck is specially designed to take the orbiter. It is only used for this job.

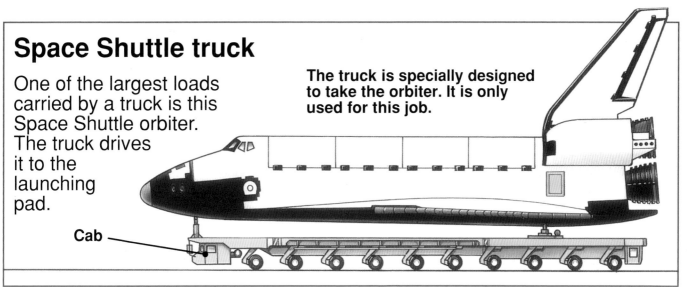

Cab

 # All-terrain truck

All-terrain trucks can drive over all sorts of ground without getting stuck. They have powerful engines and thick wheels. Their bodies are extra strong to stop them from getting damaged by rocky ground. This truck can load and unload itself, too.

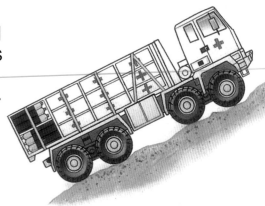

This truck can go up steep slopes, even with a heavy load.

Unloading

Rack

A metal arm lifts the rack and pushes it back until it touches the ground.

Arm

The truck drives out from underneath it.

Loading

The arm lifts the rack.

To load again, the arm lifts up the rack and the truck drives back under it.

The truck drives away.

Then the arm pulls the rack up onto the truck's body and it is ready to drive away.

The load sits on a frame called a rack.

This truck is taking medical supplies across a desert. For most of the way there are no proper roads.

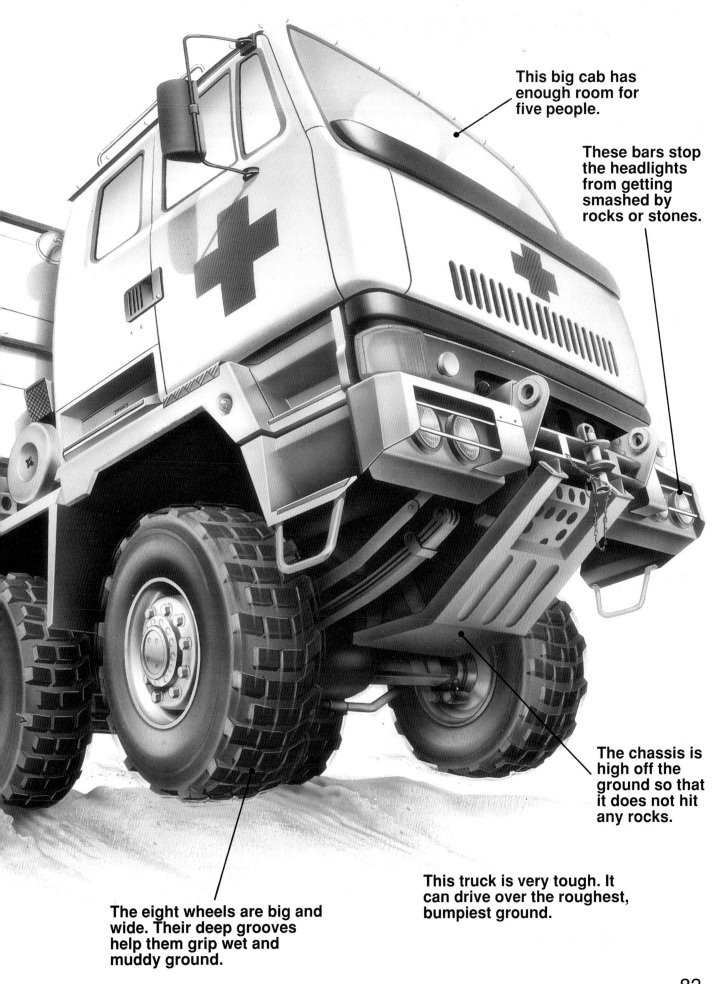

This big cab has enough room for five people.

These bars stop the headlights from getting smashed by rocks or stones.

The chassis is high off the ground so that it does not hit any rocks.

This truck is very tough. It can drive over the roughest, bumpiest ground.

The eight wheels are big and wide. Their deep grooves help them grip wet and muddy ground.

Customized truck

This big truck has some of its outside parts covered in metals called chrome and stainless steel. These are very shiny, so they look good. Trucks with extra decoration like this are called customized trucks.

The driver has put extra lights on the cab for decoration.

Fumes from the engine come out here. It is called an exhaust stack.

Stainless steel

Cab shapes

Bonnet

Engine

This truck has its engine in front of the cab, under a cover called a bonnet.

Engine

This truck has its cab on top of the engine. It is called a cab-over truck.

The tractor unit is very long. It rides smoothly over bumpy roads, so it is more comfortable for the driver.

Big loads

These big trucks are powerful. They can pull all sorts of heavy loads in different types of semi-trailers. They often go on very long journeys.

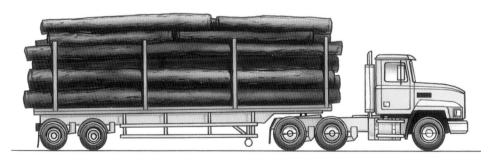

This truck is loaded with tree trunks.

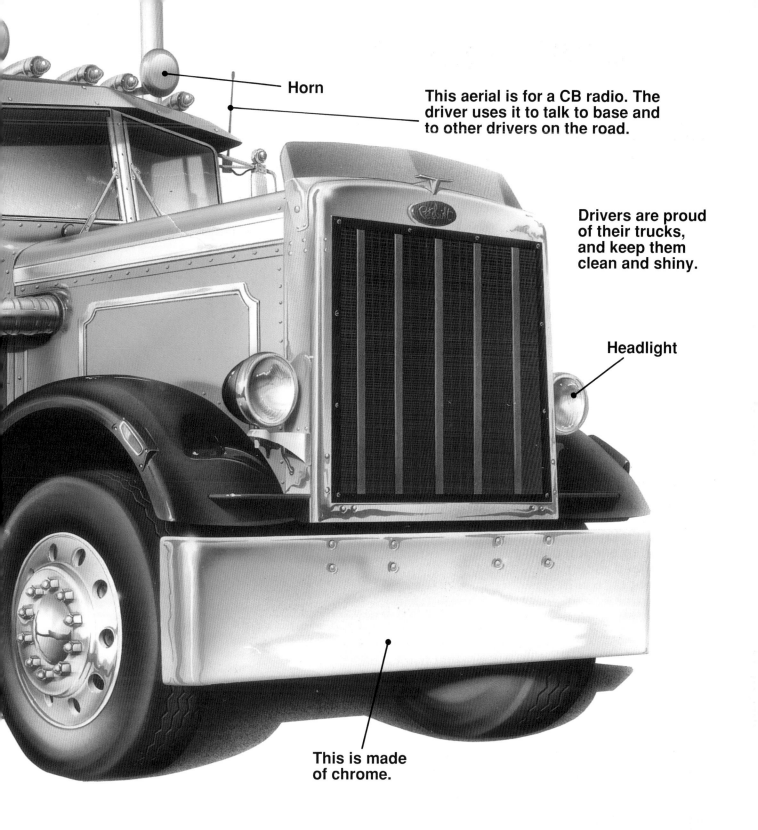

Horn

This aerial is for a CB radio. The driver uses it to talk to base and to other drivers on the road.

Drivers are proud of their trucks, and keep them clean and shiny.

Headlight

This is made of chrome.

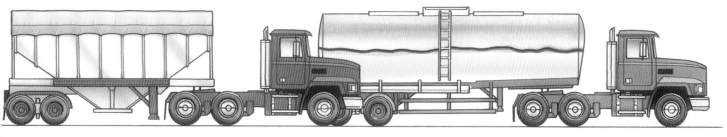

This truck's semi-trailer is full of sand.   This truck is a giant tanker (see page 70).

Pro-jet truck

This is a racing truck. It is built for speed alone, so it is not used for carrying loads like normal trucks. It is called the Pro-jet truck because it has a jet engine taken from a fighter plane.

This truck has more pulling power than an express train.

These tubes have parachutes inside. They open out to help the truck slow down.

The Pro-jet races on its own to see if it can beat speed records. It does not race with other trucks.

The Pro-jet is about 100 times more powerful than a normal truck.

Truck racing

Sometimes the tractor units of normal trucks race against each other.

The drivers have to be very skilful to control the trucks when they are going fast.

After going at top speed, it takes the truck about 500m (550yds) to be able to stop.

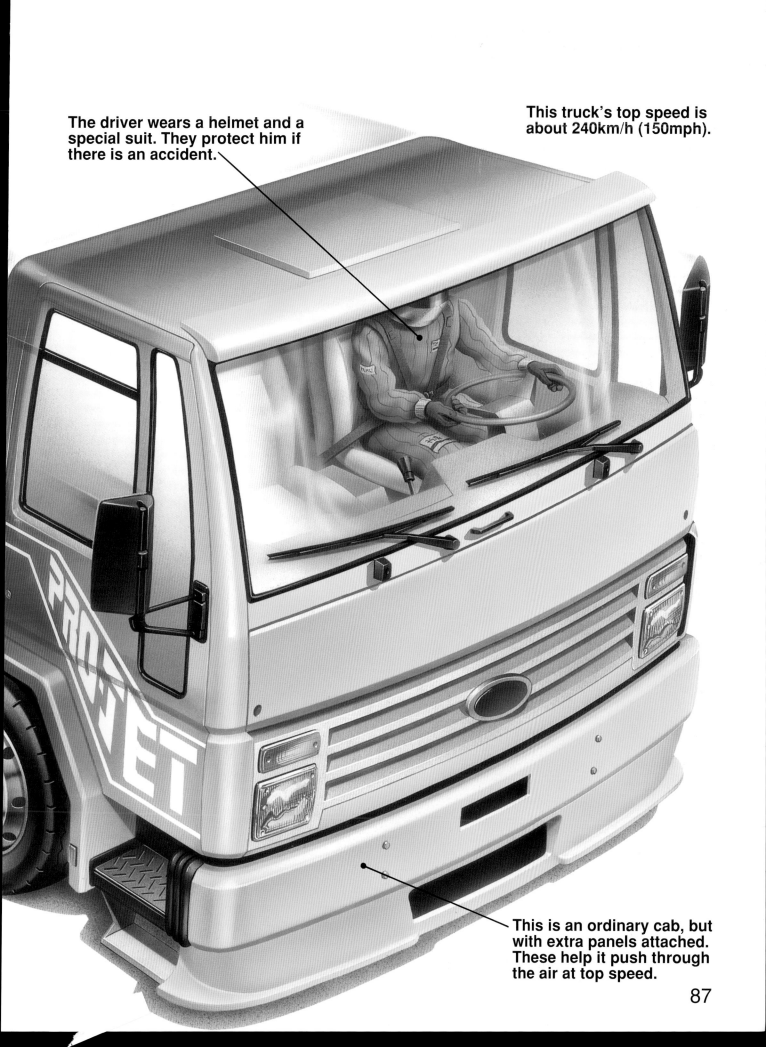

The driver wears a helmet and a special suit. They protect him if there is an accident.

This truck's top speed is about 240km/h (150mph).

This is an ordinary cab, but with extra panels attached. These help it push through the air at top speed.

 # Fire truck

Trucks are very important in firefighting. They rush the firefighters to the fire. All the equipment they need is on board.

They have loud sirens for when they are in a hurry. These warn traffic on the roads to let them pass.

Special jobs

This all-terrain (see page 82) fire truck is used where driving is difficult, such as in forests and deserts.

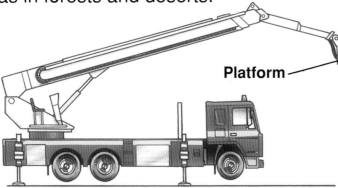

Platform

This fire truck raises and lowers a platform on its metal arm. It can reach up to the windows of tall buildings.

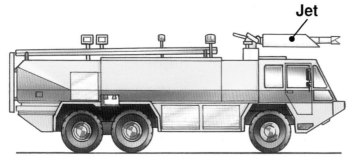

Jet

This fire truck stands by at the airport in case there is an accident. It has a strong water jet on the roof.

There is a tank inside the truck. It carries water for putting out the flames.

Ladders are kept on the roof. They are used for rescuing people.

This arm can stretch up very high. Its bright lights help the firefighters if it is dark or smoky.

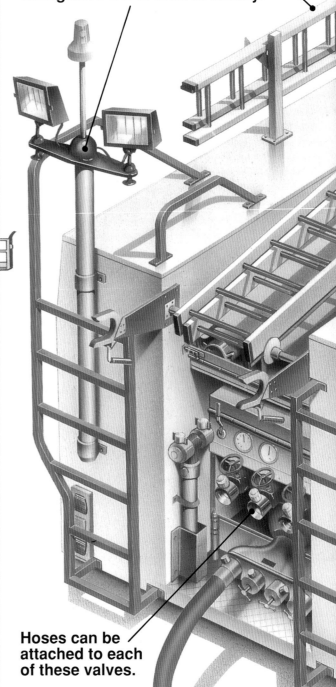

Hoses can be attached to each of these valves.

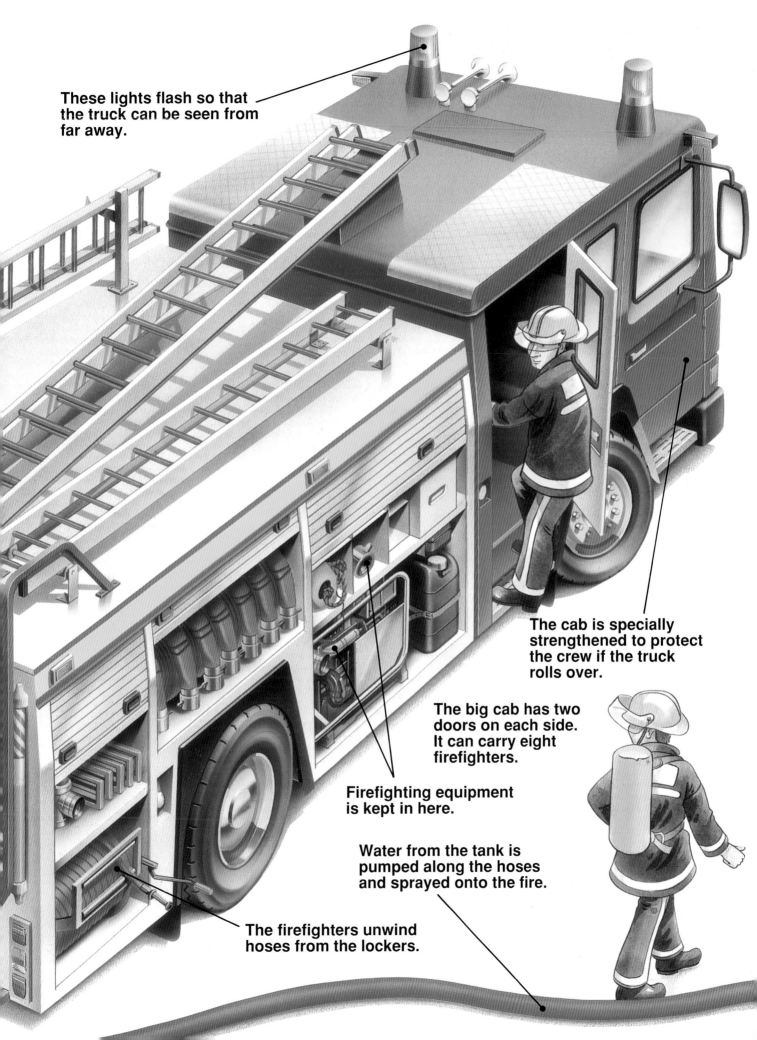

These lights flash so that the truck can be seen from far away.

The cab is specially strengthened to protect the crew if the truck rolls over.

The big cab has two doors on each side. It can carry eight firefighters.

Firefighting equipment is kept in here.

Water from the tank is pumped along the hoses and sprayed onto the fire.

The firefighters unwind hoses from the lockers.

Snowblower

In winter, this truck helps clear the roads so that other traffic can get through. It churns up the snow and blows it onto the side of the road.

This truck has powerful lights to help the driver see at night.

The snow blows out of these chutes.

This drum turns around very fast. Its blades churn up the snow.

The driver can make the drum turn at different speeds.

The snowblower has two engines. One drives the truck along and the other turns the drum.

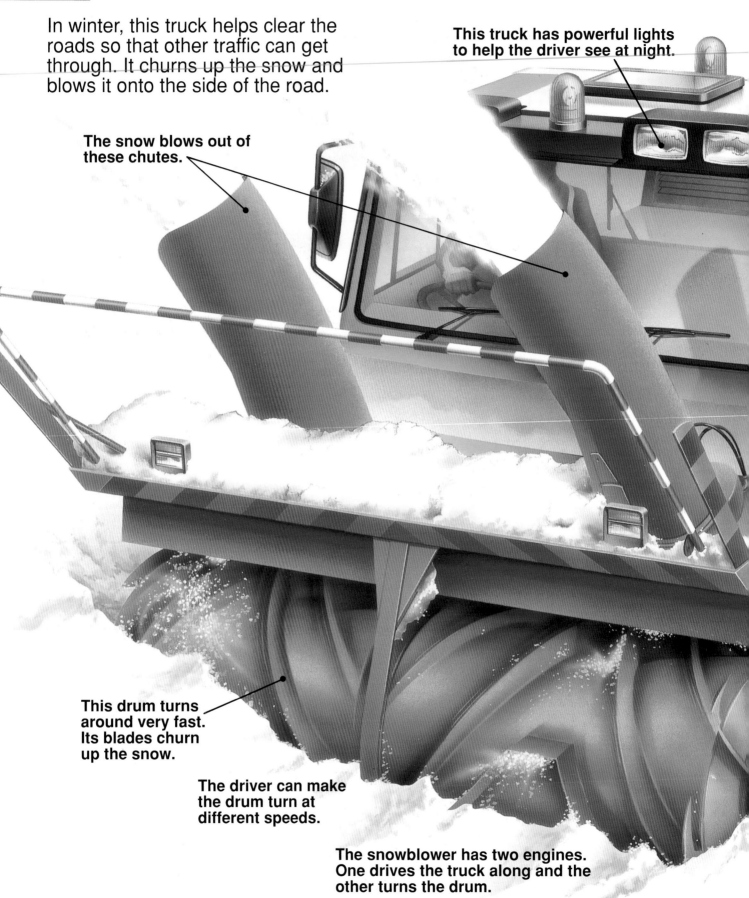

The cab is heated to keep the driver warm.

As the truck moves along, it clears a path through the snow.

How it works

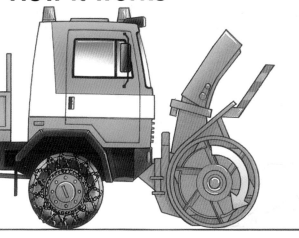

The drum's blades cut into the snow. As they spin, they fling the snow upward very hard.

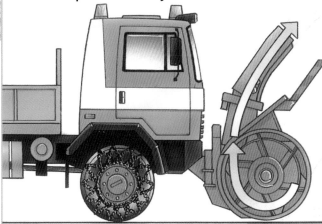

The snows flies out of the chutes. The truck moves forward, taking in more snow.

These chains stop the wheels from slipping on the snow.

The cab has thick windows. These help block out noise from the engines and the blower.

Snow plough

A snow plough clears snow by pushing it out of the way. It has a curved panel on the front called a face-plate.

Trucks from the past

Being a truck driver now is very different from seventy years ago. Trucks then were slower and less comfortable to ride in. They could not carry as much, either.

Delivery truck

This truck was built in the 1930s. The front of it looks very like the cars that were built at the same time.

Steam truck

This truck was built in 1925. When it pulls its trailer, it can only travel at 8km/h (5mph), which is about the same speed as jogging.

This truck is driven by a steam engine. It gets its power by burning coal.

The driver has to work this small wiper by hand.

The headlights stand out at the sides.

Bumpy ride

Early tyres were made of metal or wood. They were very bumpy to ride on.

Later, tyres were made of solid rubber.

Now tyres are filled with air, which cushions any bumps.

The driver has to turn this handle to start the engine.

This sheet is all that protects the load.

This truck is carrying bananas. Compare it with the truck on page 4.

The boxes have to be loaded and unloaded by hand.

The engine is in front of the cab, under a bonnet (see page 84).

Other trucks to spot

There are many different types of trucks to spot. How many can you find? What jobs are they doing? Here are some of the trucks you might see.

Skip truck

Trucks like this have containers on the back called skips or roll-offs. They collect waste from building sites.

Gully emptier

In many countries, you can see gully emptiers clearing the gullies, or drains, at the side of the road. They suck up the dirt through a long hose.

Concrete mixer and pumper

This truck carries concrete inside its body, and then pumps it to where it is needed.

Crane truck

There is a crane on the back of this truck for loading and unloading. The driver works it with levers behind the cab.

Street cleaner

This truck sweeps and washes the streets. It is small, so that it can clean narrow streets and pathways.

95

Index

With special thanks to: Commercial Motor magazine, Paul Chiltern, Peter Cramer, CSS Promotions Ltd, Adrian Graves, Robert Harris at Shell, Richard Hornsby, Steve Murty, NASA, John Philips, Pirelli, RARDE, Truck magazine, Williams Grand Prix Engineering Ltd.